THERE'S JUST NO RESISTING...

Cole Martinez

6'2", tough and toned
blue eyes, brown hair
intense and serious
an expert bodyguard
a reliable baby-sitter in a pinch
and an all-American Latin lover!

**It's American Romance with more passion,
more intensity...
and more male sex appeal!**

Dear Reader,

Last year I wrote the launch book for Harlequin American Romance's wildly popular THE ULTIMATE... miniseries. *They're the One!* featured Joseph Castillo, truly a man who epitomizes every woman's fantasy, but only one woman's dream come true. And for all of you who've written and asked for Raquel's and Antonio's stories, I'm thrilled to bring you the first book in my TALL, DARK & IRRESISTIBLE miniseries.

Raquel Santiago, the proper heiress who jilted a royal prince at the altar, is on a quest. She's free and determined to experience life to its fullest...and she's shaking up a certain bodyguard's composure while she's at it! I had great fun writing about Raquel, and I hope you'll enjoy TALL, DARK & IRRESISTIBLE. Watch for Antonio's story next month: *The Playboy & the Mommy.*

I love to hear from readers. Please write to me at P.O. Box 2704-262, Huntington Beach, CA 92647.

Warmest Regards,

Mindy Neff

The Virgin & Her Bodyguard

MINDY NEFF

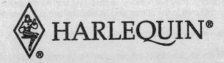

HARLEQUIN®

TORONTO • NEW YORK • LONDON
AMSTERDAM • PARIS • SYDNEY • HAMBURG
STOCKHOLM • ATHENS • TOKYO • MILAN • MADRID
PRAGUE • WARSAW • BUDAPEST • AUCKLAND

ISBN 0-373-16795-4

THE VIRGIN & HER BODYGUARD

Copyright © 1999 by Mindy Neff.

Visit us at www.romance.net

Printed in U.S.A.

To Vicky Rich

You were there when the first crazy idea was hatched, and now look where we are! Who would have thought...? Through families, kids and grandkids, trials and triumphs, you've made the last twenty years extraspecial. Thanks, my friend.

Chapter One

Cole Martinez was damned good at his job. He could track anybody or anything and had keen instincts that had never failed him. It wasn't like him to question himself, but he did so now. Surely he was in the wrong place.

He checked the address again. The cottage in the small French village perched along the hills above Nice was the right one, but the sight that greeted him wasn't.

Nor was the woman.

He'd expected jet-black hair flowing past a trim waist. He had mistakenly assumed she'd be wearing a timeless suit in neutral colors with sensible pumps.

But Raquel Santiago didn't hold up to any of his expectations. She'd cut her long hair to shoulder length and added some deep-red highlights. Pushed behind her ears, it flipped slightly at the ends. She wore a man's shirt, with the tail hanging almost to her knees, and a pair of skintight stretch pants.

Stunned by the beautiful heiress's casual, bohemian appearance, it was a moment before his senses registered the rest of the scene. Her cottage, which he now realized doubled as a photography studio, was filled with baby paraphernalia. A crib, painted candy-stripe white and red, was pushed against the far wall. Two mismatched rocking chairs sat beneath open windows draped in lace that fluttered lazily in the gentle September breeze. Toys were strewn about the hardwood floors, spilling out of a mesh-sided playpen.

In the corner there were oversize stuffed animals in a rainbow of pastels nestled against a bed of green cotton. And in the center was a baby, completely covered in pink fuzz with only its tiny round face peeking out of the costume. It was the cutest thing Cole had ever seen.

He leaned against the doorjamb and watched as Raquel snapped pictures and all but stood on her head to entertain the infant. He admired her skill and once again felt that tickling of surprise.

He had no doubt she'd balk when he stated his mission—to bring her home to their small nation of Valldoria, where she could be properly protected.

And though he could spend a lifetime just watching the enigmatic dynamo work, time was wasting.

Pushing away from the doorway, he moved into the room, making a mental note to speak with her about leaving her front door wide open. Engrossed in snapping pictures—and shaking her sweet tush to the beat of Madonna's latest hits—Raquel Santiago hadn't yet realized anyone had breached her sanctuary.

That is, until his second step landed on a rubber alligator that let out a dual-pitched, grating squeak.

Cole froze as the baby amid the stuffed animals turned wide, startled eyes on him. In delayed reaction, the infant's eyes widened and its tiny face crumbled as it began to wail.

The day was going downhill fast.

Raquel whipped around, nearly losing hold of her

prized camera. Her heart tripped as she stared at the man just inside the doorway. Tall and dark, he had a half smile on his face, an expression she knew from past experience that he used when he was determined to sway someone to his way of thinking. A man who was dynamite to look at, but a definite thorn in her side.

Cole Martinez.

"*Dios mio!* You gave me a fright! What do you want?" Though her insides quaked with emotions that weren't entirely based on surprise, she carefully stepped between the stuffed animals and lifted baby Carmen, soothing the fur-covered infant. "There, there, *ma chérie,* do not cry." Her native Latin accent gave the French words a smoky quality that got the baby's attention.

It evidently got Cole's, too, because he still hadn't spoken. He just stared.

"Why have you come, Cole?" she asked again.

"To escort you home."

Raquel shook her head, grateful that the child in her arms masked her trembling. Absurdly, Cole had always set her system off balance. "In case you had not noticed, I am in the middle of something here." She reached for the remote and turned down the stereo.

He tossed the toy alligator in the air and caught it, his large palm squeezing another squeak out of it, and casually leaned one broad shoulder against the wall. "I'll wait," he said pleasantly.

The intensity of his blue eyes—compliments of the American genes on his mother's side—speared her, rooting her to the spot. He wore a deep-charcoal suit with a French-blue dress shirt and Windsor-knotted tie. Always proper, Cole Martinez would definitely look out of place in this artisan town. Her phone would be ringing any minute now with neighbors wanting to know who the stranger was.

Shifting the baby in her arms, she arched a brow. "You will have a very long wait, I think. I have no intention of returning to Valldoria any time soon." Perversely, she hit the volume increase button on the stereo's remote.

"Rebellion," he murmured.

"Independence," she countered.

He set the plastic alligator on a table and moved around the room, still keeping an eye on her, making her even more nervous. She tried to ignore him, to look busy, and wondered if he noticed that she was failing miserably.

Probably. Not much got past Cole Martinez. There was a toughness beneath the civilized veneer. She was fairly certain a shoulder harness and gun rested underneath his tailored suit jacket. The man was both sharp and deadly. And way too predatory for her comfort level.

"I wonder," he mused, "whether it was rebellion or independence that made you jilt a royal prince at the altar."

Her heart did a funny tumble. It had been six months, but she was still surprised at herself. She'd never done anything so daring in her life. Brought up to be oh-so-correct, with never a hair out of place, running off to pursue art in lieu of marrying the prince she'd been betrothed to since birth had taken courage she hadn't known she possessed.

"Neither," she answered. With the child on her hip, she repositioned her tripod to catch the best light, wondering if she could get a few more shots before baby Carmen's mother returned. "Anyone could see that Briana and Prince Joseph were in love. I did the nice thing and made the path clear for them.''

''At the expense of your family's displeasure.''

She shrugged. ''They will get over it.''

''True. They are no longer upset but they would like you to return.''

''No.''

His brows drew together. He reached over and turned down the stereo's volume. ''Do you think Madonna is appropriate for a child's ears?''

''Carmen does not understand the words. It is the beat she responds to.''

''As do you.''

She realized she was moving her hips in time with ''I'd Rather Be Your Lover,'' and abruptly stopped. She felt her face flame when she focused on the lyrics. The half smile on Cole's lips told her he, too, was responding to the suggestive words.

Impatiently, she fiddled with her lens cap. ''State the rest of your business, Cole. I am busy and I need to get on with it.''

''I don't remember this testy side of you.''

''You never knew the sides of me.''

''You might be surprised by how much I knew.''

Growing irritated now, she blew out a breath, taking care not to squeeze Carmen in her agitation. The very softness of his voice sent chills up her spine and made her heart pound. If she didn't know better, she would suspect him of coming on to her.

And that made her uneasy. All her life, people were nice to her because they *had* to be. She was an heiress from a prominent family—practically royalty in its own right. She'd learned a tough lesson with Lucian, though.

He'd supported her love of art, given her the courage to leave Valldoria. She'd thought he'd cared about *her*.

They'd agreed to meet up in France, made plans to become famous artists, Lucian a painter, Raquel a photographer.

But when her father, Carlos Santiago, had thrown such a fit at her disappearance and insisted he would disinherit her, Lucian had shown his true colors and bolted without even unpacking his bags. He'd wanted her money. Not her. He'd been nice to her for a reason.

And because of that experience, Raquel was wary and on guard. Now, with Cole, she intended to double those walls. He was head of the Royal Guard, a trusted confidant of both King Marcos of Valldoria and her own father. It had always been his job to protect her. It was what he was *paid* to do.

She cautioned herself not to forget that, especially in light of these ridiculous fluttering sensations just his mere presence caused.

She didn't *need* or want a man. Period.

At last—after twenty-five years of chafing against strict custom and a sheltered existence that had schooled her to cater to a man's every whim—her life was now full and exciting.

And free.

Cole's unexpected appearance threatened her freedom. And that, she wouldn't abide.

"You did not come all the way to France from Valldoria to play innuendo games with me, I am sure."

"No."

"Then what do you want?"

"Unrest surrounds your father of late, and there is a possibility that the danger could spill over onto you. I have been sent to bring you home."

She was afraid of that. Raquel dismissed the danger to herself with an airy wiggle of her fingers. "If my father is threatened, why are you not there to guard him?"

"He's in good hands, I assure you. And I'll be glad to add my own capable hands to the job just as soon as you pack a bag or two." He checked the platinum watch at his wrist. "The jet is waiting at Nice airport."

"Then you must run along so you do not miss your flight."

He wasn't a man easily dismissed. She should have remembered that from the days when she'd tried to escape the family estate unescorted. She remembered it now, though. Especially when he advanced on her like a panther stalking its prey.

Like a true coward, she shifted the baby in her arms, using her as a buffer. One of his dark brows arched, but he did not stop his advance.

Her heart pounded and her insides tumbled. Girlhood fantasies teased her, embarrassed her. She'd watched him plenty of times, from her window, or from the corner of her eye as he'd fall into step beside her. She'd deliberately ducked him on more than one occasion in Valldoria. It had been a sport rife with sensuality—the sensuality being all on her part, images conjured in a sheltered young woman's mind. Daydreams of a powerful man, of those strong hands reaching for her.

She could not duck him now. There was nowhere to run. Though she felt a deep-seated urge to at least *attempt* to run, her feet did not heed the mental command.

Softly now, the music wound a sensual spell around them. The air in the simple cottage became charged with something...something musky...something she could not put a name to, had no experience with.

He stopped in front of her, the warmth of his body carrying his unique scent right to her senses, turning her knees rubbery. Her mouth went dry as his deep, whisky voice wrapped around her.

"You will not always have a child to hide behind, little spitfire."

For the life of her, she couldn't seem to look away from those penetrating blue eyes. She might not have a lot of experience, but she knew a sexual threat when she heard one. That it had come from Cole Martinez held her rooted to the spot in astonishment. Possibilities flitted through her mind, scenarios that sent her blood pulsing through her veins so fast, so hot, she felt dizzy.

There had been a time when she would have given anything to have Cole Martinez look at her just like this, a time when she'd imagined him to be her knight, her savior who'd rescue her from the smothering influence of her family, who'd climb the tower walls from the magical rungs of her long hair and declare his intentions. But that was a lifetime ago. She was a different person now. Her own person.

She saw his gaze shift, saw heat and purpose as he focused on her mouth. Breath suspended in her lungs. *Yes!* she wanted to scream. *Do it!*

Baby Carmen let out a squeal that broke the spell, reaching her little fur covered arms in the direction of the door.

Horrified by her thoughts—especially with a baby in her arms—Raquel jumped back from Cole, knowing good and well there was a guilty flush to her cheeks.

A fact that was confirmed by Sasha St-Pierre's dancing expression. "Pardon, *s'il vous plaît*. Am I interrupting?"

Raquel stepped around Cole and moved toward Carmen's young mother. "No," she said, pleased that her voice actually worked. Whatever had passed between her and Cole a moment ago had sent her into a mental tizzy. "I am finished shooting for the day. The light is no longer right, but I have enough photos for this segment." Undoing the costume fastenings, she slipped the fur suit off the baby and cuddled the warm infant before passing her to her mother.

"Who is the stranger in the Armani?" Sasha whispered with a conspiring smile. The neighbors were always trying to fix Raquel up and despaired that she did not seem interested.

"An acquaintance from my country," Raquel replied.

"He has the look of a hungry suitor to me."

Raquel arched her brow. "You have been sniffing too many of your delicacies if you must characterize everyone as being hungry."

"That is not the type of hunger I meant."

Raquel stared at her friend blankly for a moment. A possible meaning jelled in her brain, but she didn't dare look at Cole to see if she was right. Instead, she pretended innocence. "Perhaps he is weary from his flight. But famished or not, he is but an acquaintance."

"Oh, you are always so evasive. Margo and I will pull the details out of you later, I think."

"There are no details to pull." She'd known Cole would cause a stir in town. And she'd known that Sasha and Margo, the owners of the bakery next door, would want to know the full story. She *hadn't* known he'd create such havoc with her hormones.

"We will see," Sasha said with an impish grin. "He is quite a specimen."

Raquel opened her mouth to utter a denial, realized

it was useless and remained silent. Cole was very easy on the eyes. He had a presence about him that would draw the attention of a nun.

"Shall I bring Carmen for the interview tomorrow?"

Still speculating on Cole's looks, it took a moment for Raquel to bring her mind back around to business. "No. Carmen is a definite for the layout. She's a love." She kissed the baby's fingers drawing a sweet giggle from the eight-month-old. "I will call you, though, when I get the schedule laid out."

Clearly Sasha was reluctant to leave, her gaze still darting surreptitiously to Cole. She pecked a friendly kiss on Raquel's cheek. "We will talk, *mon ami*. Very soon."

Raquel watched Sasha leave with baby Carmen. Unable to stall any longer, she turned back to Cole.

"Do your neighbors always walk in unannounced?"

"Yes. Especially when I have their baby."

"That is not a good practice."

"You walked in unannounced."

"Precisely my point. Your lack of common sense regarding your security makes me realize I've come just in the nick of time."

"Do not be ridiculous. This is a small town. I have many friends. Safety is not an issue."

"Safety is *always* an issue where you are concerned."

"No. It is not. Not here. I am not Raquel Santiago, the heiress. I am merely a friend, neighbor and businesswoman."

"I can't believe your attitude. You were brought up to be careful. You were never unescorted—except when you gave us the slip," he said dryly.

Raquel shrugged and dismantled her camera equipment. "It was a game." She hadn't meant to admit that, was afraid he'd pounce on the words and ask for clarification. Cole Martinez loved to ask questions.

In Valldoria he was always there whenever she tried to step out of the fortress, there to remind her of her duty and her place. He was obsessive about her security in a quiet, steely sort of way. Yet he seemed to get a kick out of watching her bristle when he fell into step beside her like a shadow. It had become a game with her, to see if she could shake him.

She couldn't very well tell him that her girlhood goal had been to provoke a reaction out of him.

A sexual reaction.

Thankfully he let the subject drop, but the speculation in his intense blue gaze told her he'd filed the incomplete data in that sharp mind of his and reserved the right to call it up at a moment's notice. She was only off the hook temporarily.

Unless she could get him out the door and back to Valldoria where he belonged.

She saw him glance at his watch again. "How much time do you need?"

"For what?"

A muscle twitched at the corner of his eye. "To pack."

"I'm not going anywhere."

She saw his chest expand as he took what she assumed was a calming breath. "Your father wishes otherwise."

"I know. That's precisely why I'm in France and not Valldoria."

"Can you not conduct your business in your home country?"

"Are you kidding? My family views my art as a

hobby. They are sure I will come to my senses. But it's not a hobby, Cole. It's my business." She had to make him understand. Her family was both powerful and persuasive. And Cole had the authority and backing to carry out their orders. She didn't want to fight him on the matter, but she would.

"So far, I am doing poster art and greeting cards—my own line. Soon, I hope to branch out, perhaps in publishing. The possibilities are unlimited."

"I appreciate that you enjoy your work, but face it, you don't need the money."

"This isn't about money. It's about freedom, self-fulfillment. Standing on my own. I am sole proprietress of my venture. I answer to no one but me."

"And that's important to you?"

"Very."

He studied her for a long moment, and she fought not to squirm.

"I imagine your name helps with sales."

"You are wrong." She nearly bent the leg of her tripod as she snapped it closed. "And I resent that insinuation. I am good at what I do, Cole."

"Ah, spitfire, you misunderstood. I didn't mean to imply that your name and status were all you had going for you. I can *see* your talent." His gaze touched on the prints of babies that hung on every available wall space. "I meant that it would be an added bonus."

"As I told you, no one here knows that I am an heiress. I have kept my background private. Here in France I am merely Mademoiselle Raquel."

"But you have the distinctive look of a beautiful, exotic *senorita* about you."

Her heart lurched and she firmly pulled back on the reins of her runaway emotions. He wanted something from her. Compliance. And she suspected he'd use any means to attain it.

"Flattery will not get you your way."

He shrugged, a half smile tipping his lips. "A man can try. I understand women like compliments."

"Sincere ones, yes—and I get plenty from the local boys of the village."

Cole felt his chest tighten. Jealousy, for crying out loud? "There is a difference between a man and a boy, Raquel. I'll be glad to demonstrate if you like." He saw her jolt, saw the fine trembling in her fingers, the slight twitch at the corner of her full mouth. But before he could feel too smug, she astonished him with her next words.

"I ought to call your bluff."

Raquel Santiago *had* grown up. He hadn't expected her to see through him. Few did. Because he didn't allow it. He must be slipping.

"You think I'm bluffing?" he asked softly, dangerously, taking a step closer, hemming her in, crowding her. He saw her nervousness, saw her fight it with the squaring of her shoulders.

"Put up or shut up, Cole Martinez." Her voice trembled, but her dark eyes were direct. Innocent eyes, asking for a taste of forbidden fruit.

And he *was* forbidden fruit. His own rules. One did *not* dally with one's charge. Especially when that charge was an heiress. She wasn't in his class. His job was to protect her.

And that included protection from himself.

Still, he couldn't seem to stop himself from responding to her challenge. Before he could check the movement, he tipped her chin up, tested the new, shorter length of her hair, rubbing the silky strands with his fingertips. Her tongue skimmed the seam of her lips, leaving them wet and alluring. The action slammed into him with the force of a rifle kick.

A game, she'd said earlier. Could Raquel Santiago be entertaining an attraction? God knows the attraction wouldn't be one-sided. He'd fantasized about this woman for more years that he cared to recall. Fantasies that were definitely off-limits.

"You're playing with fire, little one."

Raquel placed a palm on his chest, felt the silk of his tie, the heat of his skin through the French-blue cotton, the pounding of his heart.

He was so close, she tasted the warmth of his breath. She'd deliberately taunted him and wondered if that was such a smart idea. He could very well be more man than she could handle. Still, she wanted to experience him. Just once. Because the opportunity would more than likely never present itself again.

"Maybe I like the heat," she said.

His blue eyes flared. She gave a slight, experimental tug to his tie. And met with resistance. As she'd half known she would. Cole was a master at evading her. It was as if he wore armor around his emotions.

Loosening her hold, she flattened her palm against his chest and gave a gentle shove. "Chicken."

Before she could even turn, Cole gripped her arm and yanked her to him, pressing her solidly against his body. She felt an instant of fear—or maybe it was excitement—before his mouth came down on hers, surprising her with his gentleness. After all, she'd prodded the tiger. It stood to reason she'd get bitten.

But his tender kiss was even more dangerous. Strong hands held her in place as his lips explored her mouth.

It was like nothing she'd ever experienced. Lucian's kisses had been dry and polite and respectful.

There was nothing polite about the way Cole kissed her. He kissed her with an expertise that had her forgetting her own name.

It was the kiss of a Latin lover. Sure and firm and no-nonsense. The type of kiss that mussed the hair and took a woman right out of herself, tapped into her femininity in no uncertain terms.

And even as these impressions surfaced, the kiss was over and he was pulling back. The unreadable mask was once again in place, and Raquel could have hit him. Her heart raced and she felt dizzy, as if she was floating. Every nerve ending she possessed screamed for more. She felt out of control.

Cole, in contrast, appeared perfectly *in* control.

She wasn't sure whether to be happy about that or scared as hell. Cole Martinez was the last man she should even consider getting involved with.

His life was in Valldoria. Hers was here in France.

Good thing he wasn't staying.

"Satisfied?" he asked roughly, giving her the impression he might not be as controlled as he appeared.

"No," she said bluntly, honestly. "But then I wasn't looking for satisfaction."

"Weren't you?"

She shrugged.

"Careful who you toy with, *senorita*. You might end up over your head."

"Not much chance of that. You'll be in Valldoria. I'll be here. Out of sight, out of mind." Yeah, fat chance after that toe-curling kiss.

"Wrong, spitfire. You're coming home with me."

"Obviously you have not been listening. I dislike repeating myself—unless, of course, it's for my sweet babies—but I will make an exception for you. No. Once and for all, no."

"Must you be so stubborn?"

She sighed, all traces of sassiness gone. "Cole, don't do this to me. I cannot go back. Not yet anyway. I'm just finding my feet. You have assured me my father is well. And I am confident that you and your men will see to it that he remains so."

"Was it that bad?"

He was asking about her upbringing. It was unseemly for a woman such as herself to mention any hint of discontent or let slip the smallest detail that could be construed as airing the Santiago dirty laundry. But Cole knew the family secrets. He was paid to know them.

"To an outsider looking in, I must seem like a spoiled brat for saying yes. But I was smothered at home, wilting. Here, I can bloom like a flower. I am thriving. You must understand."

Cole raked a hand through his hair. Perhaps he did understand. She was definitely different. A happy glow surrounded her. But that didn't solve his problem. "There is a matter of your safety."

"I am safe here."

"Oh yeah? What about your open doors? I walked in and was here several minutes before you even noticed. What if I'd intended you harm?" He'd done much worse. He'd kissed her, given himself a taste of what he could not have.

"I have only to yell and the neighbors will come to my aid."

"What if they're not home?"

"Margo and Sasha operate the bakery. Someone is always there. Otherwise the village would starve."

He didn't respond to her teasing. "I have orders not to leave you unguarded."

"I do not need a baby-sitter. Consider your orders rescinded."

"Sorry, spitfire. You don't have that authority."

Her breath actually hissed. "If you are worried about job security, I shall speak to my father."

"No. You shall not." Clearly he was affronted, and she didn't really blame him. It was a reminder of their differences. He worked for her father, and that gave her a certain amount of power over him. In theory only. No one really had power over Cole Martinez. He was a force unto himself. And because of that, he wouldn't like her pulling rank on him—assuming that was even possible.

"It appears we are at an impasse." For her own self-respect, she could not give in. And Cole didn't appear ready to budge, either. "What now?" she asked.

"I'll stay here."

"You will not." The very thought of such a notion sent her hormones straight back into a tizzy. As though it had a mind of its own, her gaze darted to the bedroom door. *Dios!* Her imagination was becoming entirely too creative.

"Two choices. You come with me, or I move in. That's as far as I'll go in negotiations."

"I *can't* come with you. I have babies scheduled for auditions tomorrow and the rest of the week. I have a deadline for this shoot, a firm business contract. I have given my word. It is impossible for me to leave."

"Then we go with plan B. I'm moving in."

"The cottage is too small." It was absurd to even consider the arrangement. And there was no excuse for the way her heart fluttered. "My guest quarters have been turned into a darkroom. Where will you sleep?"

"The couch will do."

She eyed his six-foot-three frame. "You will not fit."

"I've slept under worse conditions."

"But it is not necessary."

"Yes. It is."

She knew finality when she heard it. She was no match to bodily throw him out. And judging by the rigid set of his square jaw and his widespread stance, that's what it would take.

So she gave in, albeit ungraciously. "Fine. Suit yourself. But stay out of my way."

Cole was so astonished by the sassy order it was a moment before he could think straight. *He* was used to giving orders. Not the other way around.

Chapter Two

Cole was a man who planned for any contingency. Although he'd expected this to be a quick return trip, he'd packed a bag just in case of delays.

He hadn't anticipated the delay being Raquel's stubbornness. Oh, he'd known she'd balk. He just hadn't been prepared for the strength of her refusal.

Nor his reaction to that impassioned refusal.

She had been taught well. She could draw herself up, and appear haughty, bored and disinterested, as if she didn't have a thought in her head. But Cole knew there was plenty that went on in that fertile mind of hers. It aggravated him that she was so willing to dismiss him—and at the same time it challenged him.

Perhaps it was high time he figured out what actually made Raquel Santiago tick. He'd watch and learn, and file the data away.

And he would *not* kiss her again.

Hell. His heart was still pounding in overdrive.

She'd disappeared into her darkroom as if he weren't even there. Not exactly the manners of a proper heiress schooled in the correctness of tea parties.

But this wasn't a tea party. Anonymous letters aimed

at the Santiago family told him the fiesta could turn deadly.

And he needed information from Raquel. Needed to know the smallest detail that might have indicated that the creeps leveling threats had honed in on Carlos's beautiful daughter. Though overprotective, it was common knowledge that Carlos Santiago doted on his only daughter.

And if Cole could track her whereabouts, so could the enemy.

He knocked on the closed door that bore a sign threatening dire consequences should anyone have the nerve to open it.

"Momento," came a sharp reply.

His jaw tightened, aching with the pressure. He wasn't a man to cool his heels with any sort of grace. He was accustomed to snapping his fingers and having his commands obeyed instantly.

His idea of "instantly" turned into several minutes. At last she yanked open the door, letting out a rush of scent, of chemicals he couldn't identify that had to do with picture developing.

"You are still here?" she demanded.

At five-foot-four—and barefoot, he noted—she barely reached his chin. He stared down at her. "I intend to be your shadow, *senorita*. Get used to it."

"I have been thinking," she said, brushing past him with a folder in her hands. "Perhaps I was too hasty with my decision to let you stay. My neighbors will form a bad impression of my character."

"There is a remedy for that."

She looked incredibly relieved. "Good, I knew you were a sensible man. You will be leaving then?"

"If you come with me."

Relief turned to annoyance. "You are a man with a one-track mind. You might consider expanding your horizons."

He'd expanded them plenty with that kiss. "I might accuse you of the same closed-mindedness."

She sat on the sofa, legs spread wide, the long tails of the man-style shirt tugged between the open V of her slender limbs. It was a slouchy position, not meant to be seductive. Nonetheless, his body responded with incendiary swiftness.

Her deportment instructor would have a fit should she see the heiress displaying such casualness, especially in the company of a man.

Cole wasn't sure his heart could take this bodyguarding stint.

"In the last six months, my mind has been very open. Look at these photographs and tell me there is no imagination."

She spread the photos on the coffee table, pride evident in the reverent way she touched each glossy. He moved beside her and sat. The smell of processing chemicals vied with her floral perfume. Their knees bumped and she jolted, scooting over a few inches. It did little good. When she leaned forward to separate the photos, her shoulder brushed his arm. The baggy shirt gaped, giving him a tantalizing view of her breasts.

Innocence, he thought. She had no idea the effect she had on him. But why would she? Theirs had never been that type of relationship. Except in his secret dreams.

Her actions were not deliberate or coy. Just simple, fresh and natural.

He dragged his gaze to safer territory—the photographs. Her skill was obvious. Children, no two expressions alike, were depicted as cherubs and hearts.

Obviously a Valentine theme. The range from innocent to impish was amazing.

"Why babies?" he asked.

"Because they never fail to evoke emotions. It just hit me one day as I was sitting at an outdoor café and a woman with twin girls sat across the way. I could not keep my eyes off those sweet infants. And neither could the other customers. Everyone smiled, young and old." She glanced at him. "Do you not automatically smile and feel a certain warmth and happiness when you see a baby?"

"In my position, I don't see babies that often."

"Oh, think, Cole. Were you not moved by Carmen? Just a little bit?"

He shrugged, feeling uncomfortable. "I suppose." Actually he had thought it was pretty cute, a little bitty face peeking out of that furry costume.

She punched him lightly on the shoulder, surprising him with the playfulness.

"Such emotion. No matter. If you stick around, I guarantee my babies will get to you. It takes but a moment for them to capture your heart."

Passionate about her subject, she didn't appear to realize that she'd just accepted his presence without argument.

"Before I knew what hit me," she continued, "the images were so strong in my mind. I asked the mother if I could photograph her children and she agreed. Once word got out, I had no lack of babies or ideas."

He glanced over to the corner of the room that doubled as her set. The cynical, cautious side of him rose. "Do you design those sets yourself?"

"Mostly. This is an artist's colony, and when I need assistance there are plenty of local enthusiasts to lend a hand. Most of my ideas and designs are simple, though.''

''Do you purchase the materials yourself or are they delivered?''

''Both.''

''When was your last delivery?''

''Two weeks ago. Why?''

''Have you ordered anything recently?''

''Probably. I order at random. I do not always keep track. Why?'' she asked again.

''I do not want you to open any package that comes. You're not to touch it in any way until I have examined it. Understand?''

Her eyes widened. ''Cole, just how serious is this threat to my father? You did say it was a mere threat?''

''No threat is *mere*. At this point though, no physical moves have been made. We are tightening security, taking preventive measures.''

''But my babies. They are not in any danger, are they? Through me?''

''I cannot guarantee that.'' Perhaps he could play on that compassion to get her to budge.

She jumped to her feet, scattering pictures in the process. ''Do not attempt to frighten me. I need to know if I am inadvertently putting these children in danger or if you are exaggerating to get me to bend to your will?''

He felt like a heel as he rescued an eight-by-ten glossy of a baby dressed as a cherub, sound asleep on a heart-shaped pillow. He doubted that Raquel or her cute photography subjects were in immediate danger here in France. Truthfully, the percentage might rise should she return to Valldoria.

But even if there was a slim possibility of danger, he needed to be prepared, to have her in his sights.

"As long as I am watching over you, your little babies will be safe."

"You are certain?"

"Yes," he said, surprised at his own arrogance. Nothing in life was guaranteed. Still, even more surprising, was how much he *wanted* to stay here.

"And my father will be safe in your absence? And Mama?"

"Yes." Here he was more sure. "They have an entire army sticking to them like glue."

"Then I apologize for my ungraciousness earlier. You are welcome to stay and guard my small cottage. It is a much better arrangement than should I return with you."

"That's not necessarily so." At least *he* would be much more comfortable if they were in Valldoria where they would have the full military at their disposal—*and* they wouldn't be forced into such close quarters.

"Cole, please understand. My life-style here has altered so drastically...." She ran a fingertip over a music box with dancing teddy bears, coaxing out several notes of a soft lullaby. "If I were to once again be thrust under lock and key I would perish."

"For crying out loud. You wouldn't be a prisoner. No one would lock you away." He didn't like the bleakness that washed over her, a transformation so powerful and swift, he could see it from across the room.

"Not physically, maybe. That was an exaggeration. But it may as well be fact."

Automatically he stood and went to her. Her fingertips were cold, her hands trembling. Her reaction was so strong it scared him.

"*Querida,* your distress unnerves me." He wasn't

good at soft words, but he tried anyway. "Did someone harm you in childhood? Are you *afraid* to go home?"

Her eyes widened. "No! Not in the way you mean. My family loves me. It's just that…"

Raquel tugged her hands from his gentle hold. How could she explain her feelings to him? It would certainly appear that she was overreacting, especially because she was brought up in a life-style where she had wanted for nothing.

Except for freedom and the right to be her own person.

"Customs can be very stifling," she said. "I was surrounded with love, but I was very lonely. I had no girlfriends—because my schedule did not allow for the time to cultivate friendships. There was also the worry of my instructors that bad habits would rub off on me, that I would pick up traits that were not befitting a princess."

She saw his gaze dart to the mess strewn across her hardwood floors and couldn't help but smile.

"Isolation and instruction does not eliminate a fertile imagination. In my solitude of my perfectly correct room, I imagined myself giggling with girlfriends, dancing with strangers and smoking in the bathroom, of all things."

"Do you?"

She laughed at his astonished expression. "No. So don't bother searching the mess for hidden ashtrays. Actually, I tried smoking once, and spent the next hour in the bathroom sick as a dog. The unpleasantness cured me of experimentation with tobacco."

"So your imagination turned to pictures?"

"Yes. I nagged Papa until he bought me a camera. There is such freedom behind the lens. The images you see, the possibilities, the beauty. I researched the entire process and taught myself all I needed to know about photography, from setting the F-stop to developing the film. I am no longer a see-and-be-seen woman who is a mere ornament with servants at my beck and call. I do my own shopping and cleaning—''

''Now *there's* where you ought to consider getting help,'' he interrupted dryly. ''This place looks as if a mad poodle got loose in here.''

''My floors are clean, even if they are messy. My friends come to see me, not my housekeeping abilities. I do not have to put on airs or keep up appearances. I am just me. And I have friends. And a business. I am happy, Cole. But I cannot guarantee that I would remain so if you were to put me back in my old environment. What if I slipped into my old shell? It took twenty-five years to break out. Six months is not so long to erase old traits.''

''You do yourself a disservice. No one viewed your old traits as bad.''

''Because I was trained to be a good actress. A robot. On the outside I was a composed package, but on the inside I was weeping. I do not want to weep anymore, Cole.''

Her brown eyes beseeched him to understand. No, this woman should not weep. She should smile, laugh…love. Something deep within him turned over, a secret door he didn't dare open and examine. Because the idea of being loved by a woman like Raquel Santiago was too temptingly bittersweet.

Especially for a man like him. A man who worked for her father. He was sworn to protect her, not get involved.

He told himself he could do his job and remain detached. Staying here in France just meant he'd have another base to cover. A few days of lost sleep would be worth it, though, in order not to extinguish Raquel Santiago's special light.

He nodded. "Very well. I will try not to invade your life-style. I'll still be staying, that part's not negotiable, but I will endeavor to be unobtrusive. You will not even know I am here."

Her smile blossomed, arrowing straight to his midsection.

"Oh, let us not get carried away. Your size alone will make your presence known. But I appreciate your offer."

He needed a few minutes to regroup, to marshal his defenses against this enigmatic woman who continued to poleax him. Going from despair to teasing like the flick of a switch was unsettling. And he wasn't a man who unsettled easily. It wouldn't do to get sloppy. Not only was his reputation on the line, lives were at stake.

He reached in his jacket pocket for the cell phone. He needed to dismiss the pilot, retrieve his travel bag, and apprise his second in command of the change in strategical plans.

TWO HOURS LATER Cole wandered into the kitchen. It wasn't a total disaster, but close to it. He kept a firm lid on his astonishment when he saw Raquel—heiress to a fortune beyond most people's wildest dreams—standing at the kitchen sink, eating cold spaghetti straight from the refrigerator container. Beside her was a sketch pad, which she made notations on between bites.

"Can't you at least stop long enough to prepare a decent meal?"

She jumped, dropping her fork in the sink. "*Dios mio!* Must you sneak?"

"I didn't sneak. I'm just naturally light on my feet."

"It is a wonder with your size." Raquel narrowed her eyes at the slight smirk on his too-handsome face. He'd taken off his suit jacket and loosened his tie. He was six-foot-three inches of solid muscle. Honed and conditioned. And just looking at him made her knees go weak. "I forgot you were here."

"Perhaps I should make it a point to leave a more lasting impression."

She realized she'd more or less punched him right in the ego. Not her intention, exactly, but it gave her a secret feminine thrill. Still, the thrill was much too dangerous.

She held up a hand when he moved purposefully toward her. "Stop right there. We must set house rules, I think."

"Those being?"

He was too close. She licked her lips. "No more kissing."

"I dare you to tell me you didn't like it," he said softly.

At times he appeared so correct and others...well, it was the other times that made her nervous. There were moments when he was far more American than Latin. She found the contrast fascinating. Now, however, he had the definite seductive aura of his Latin heritage, that unique, exclusive look that spoke directly to her femininity like a shout.

And it made her bold.

"You dare me?"

"Mmm." His fingertips lightly brushed the curve of her jaw.

"Ah, Senor Martinez. But I *did* like your kiss. Very much."

Cole felt his chest expand. The leather straps of his shoulder harness and weapon cut into his armpits. This enigmatic woman had a way of tripping him up in his own web. "You are quite different from the girl I remember."

"Thank you. I will consider that a compliment of the highest order."

"Surely you don't lack for compliments."

"I am not fishing. I look in the mirror every day and I know what I see. The exterior package can be made beautiful when you know the tricks. I spent years learning those tricks. So, you comment on my looks and I dismiss it. You tell me I am different and I rejoice. Because you are referring to the *inner* me."

"I suspect that inner you has always been there. She just wasn't allowed to come out."

Raquel grinned. "And now she has run amok, you are thinking?"

He responded to her grin with one of his own. "Well, she could benefit from a housekeeper."

"Are you applying for the job?"

He shook his head, sorely tempted to kiss that enticing mouth. Which would be a big mistake. If he kissed her again, he might not stop. "My talents lie more in military than domestic."

"Then you must look the other way. We are on my turf now. If you do not find the accommodations up to standard, please feel free to search elsewhere."

She sidestepped him and turned to rinse her fork under the tap, leaving a trail of water droplets on the floor as she aimed the utensil toward the dishwasher. The plastic container went back in the fridge, its lid on crooked.

Cole cringed. His sense of orderliness was definitely offended.

"Oh!" Raquel said. Evidently remembering her manners, she jerked the bowl of spaghetti back out, sending the lid sailing like a Frisbee straight for him.

He bent and picked up the lid. The woman was hell on a man's ego.

"Sorry," she said. "Did you want some?"

He stepped closer, inspected it. "Homemade?"

"Yes. The butcher's wife, Eloise, cooks for me sometimes."

"Smells good." He was relieved to hear someone was a competent cook. At least he wouldn't starve. "I'll heat it up. Do you have anything to go with it?"

She peered in the crisper. "Afraid not. This lettuce looks pitiful—" The doorbell chime stopped her in midsentence. Cole instantly went on alert.

"Come in!" Raquel shouted.

"Woman," Cole muttered, "have you lost your mind? Stay put."

He stepped through the arched passageway, one hand already covering the gun strapped to the harness at his back.

The door opened with such force, it slammed against the wall.

Adrenaline surged like a flash point, yet Cole went deadly calm. Instincts honed by years of training kicked in.

Before the door had even made a rebound, he'd palmed his thirty-eight.

"Freeze!"

Chapter Three

A statuesque woman with a full head of carrot-red hair came to an abrupt halt. The fragrant basket of rolls scattered as her hands shot up in surrender.

The next thing Cole knew, all hell had broken loose.

The carrot-top bombshell screamed. Raquel rushed past him like a whirlwind and no fewer than eight people poured in the door.

Like a tiny barricade, Raquel planted herself between Cole and the mob—customers at the bakery, he learned when everyone began talking at once—who were responding to the redhead's alarm.

"Everything is fine," Raquel said. She whipped around and glared at Cole. "Would you put that gun away before poor Margo has a heart attack?"

He holstered the weapon—reluctantly. It made him jumpy to have this many strangers in the room. And the noise level was deafening. "Do you know *all* these people?"

"Of course. They are neighbors."

"I thought you could use some rolls," Margo said faintly, a hand covering her heaving bosom. "I know how you are about forgetting to eat."

"Thank you, Margo. You are a love to think of me when you have a shop full of customers."

Having gotten herself under control, the woman drew herself up and studied Cole as if he were a rabid wolf about to eat her precious lamb. "Who is this man, Raquel? And why does he have a gun?"

"He is an acquaintance from my country." Concerned that Cole was outnumbered, Raquel moved a little closer to him.

"But he has a gun!" Margo reiterated with French dramatics, causing a murmur to buzz through the crowd. Several of the male gender did a little muscle flexing.

Cole flexed back, she noticed. Wonderful. She needed to clear the room. Fast. Before the combined level of testosterone got totally out of hand.

She knew full well Sasha had sent Margo to poke around for details.

She just wasn't ready to give those details.

She enjoyed her anonymity. If her friends learned of her background, they would very likely treat her differently—and the joy of at last having girlfriends was too cherished to chance ruining.

Although if she didn't attempt to run some damage control, these friendships might very well already be on the way to ruin. Especially now, in light of Cole pulling a gun on the woman as if she were a criminal on the Most Wanted list.

Raquel pasted a teasing smile on her face.

"Latin men," she scoffed, linking her arm through Cole's. "They are hot-blooded and hair-triggered." From the corner of her eye, she saw his brow raise at her characterization but ignored him. "Cole is not used to company entering at will and he becomes nervous. And I believe he must be punchy from his flight. He will be more civilized tomorrow, after he has rested on my couch.''

''He is staying with you?'' Thomas, the butcher, asked.

She felt Cole stiffen and pinched his arm, keeping her smile in place. ''On the sofa, Tom,'' she stressed. ''He brings news of my family, and we have much to discuss. So you see? Everything is fine. And quite platonic.''

''You are sure?'' Margo asked.

''She is sure,'' Cole answered, his voice soft and whisky smooth. ''My apologies, *madame*, for giving you a fright.''

Margo fluffed her hair and tugged her skintight blouse over her ample bosom. ''It is *mademoiselle*.''

''Pardon me. Nice to make your acquaintance… Mademoiselle St-Pierre. As Senorita Raquel has said, I will be more civilized tomorrow.''

''Quit while you're ahead,'' Raquel warned, her voice pitched for his ears alone. Then she gathered up the rolls, placed them back in the basket and displayed the innate skills of a proper heiress as she graciously thanked each person for coming so quickly. She asked after each of their families and traded jokes with a few.

With the chaos defused, the neighbors departed and she shut the door, leaving just the two of them.

He expected sparks from her snapping brown eyes and she didn't disappoint him.

''I cannot believe you did that!''

''What's not to believe? You know damned well I'm trained to draw first and ask questions later. I don't know these people. Any one of them could have intended you harm.''

''They are my neighbors! Now word will get out and

parents will be reluctant to bring their babies. I will not have you ruining my business!'' She thrust out her hand. ''You must give me that horrible gun.''

''Not on your life, spitfire. I don't surrender my weapon to anyone.''

''Then you must leave.''

''You know my conditions for leaving.''

Although his stance was loose and easy, she didn't kid herself. He had that look about him that told her he wasn't about to budge. She nearly stamped her foot—an action that would have horrified her mother.

''Guns and babies do not mix, Cole. If you insist on being underfoot, there is a chance you might have to hold one of the little ones. It will not do to poke their sweet hides with that cold steel!'' If she hadn't been so worked up, she might have laughed at the horror that crossed his face.

''I assure you, I have no intention of holding a kid. That's what mothers are for.''

''And there is the next problem. They will see that you are armed and think you are a madman! No one will trust me with their child!''

''Calm down. I've apologized. I know how to be discreet.''

She actually snorted. ''One would not know it from your behavior this night.''

''I'm having an off day,'' he muttered.

''What was that?''

''I said, can I stay?'' That threw her off track, he noticed. Her dark brows, arched by nature and a skillful use of tweezers, lowered.

''You are asking? Mr. obey-my-orders, don't-mess-with-me Martinez is actually asking? Are you unwell? Shall I call the *medicos?*''

"Cute," he grumbled. The smell of fresh baked bread reminded him he hadn't eaten. And if the truth be told, he felt a twinge of embarrassment for overreacting with the buxom Margo. "If I warm the spaghetti, will you share those rolls?"

"Ah, not ill, I see. Merely hungry. You are awfully certain I will agree to you staying."

"Certainty is my business."

"A business you are obviously quite poor at."

"I beg your pardon?"

"Certainty does not have you pointing a gun at my innocent neighbors."

"Lighten up, spitfire. What would you have me do when a door crashes nearly off its hinges as though someone's rushing the guard?"

"Margo had her hands full with the rolls. And the door sticks on occasion. That is why I leave it standing wide—"

"You won't be doing that anymore."

"—open. So the force she used is understandable. I am used to the sound."

"Well I'm not. Are you going to share those rolls or make me go next door and take my chances with the rescue mob?"

She studied him for a moment. There was a weary cast to his blue eyes. She knew he was dedicated to his work and wondered when last he had slept. Compassion nudged her, especially since he *had* actually been accommodating. After all, she was still in France. Free. With wonderful anticipation of the baby auditions that would begin tomorrow.

She, too, could be accommodating. To a point. "If you warm the meal, you will dirty a pan."

"You mean to tell me you eat cold food so you won't have to do dishes?"

"I happen to like cold spaghetti. Growing up, it would have been a terrible breach of etiquette to eat it that way."

"Rebellion," he stated. "You are determined to experience every little thing that was denied to you. I'll sweeten the pot. I'll warm *and* do the dishes."

She grinned and thrust the basket of rolls in his hands. "You have a deal."

SHE STOOD in the front room, her arms full of extra blankets and pillows. Now that the time had come to assign sleeping arrangements, she felt uncommonly edgy. She'd never spent the night with a man before. Never mind that they would be in separate rooms. Cole Martinez's presence was all-encompassing.

She watched him prowl around her tiny cottage, his expression growing grimmer by the minute. When he saw her hovering just inside the room, he sent her a scowl.

"You might as well invite the enemy in for a tea party. The locks on your doors and windows are a joke. Not that you actually use them," he added with a censorious shake of his head.

Here she was entertaining sexual nerves and he was back in true form…bristling. She should have saved the energy. After all, other than that kiss earlier, he had never shown any interest in having designs on her person. Those had only been *her* fantasies.

Steadier now, she squared her shoulders and walked across the room. "You saw for yourself the army of people who came instantly to my rescue. We have a safe and protective neighborhood. Besides, the tourist season is winding down and our village will soon be the sleepy little artist town we cherish so."

"You're too trusting. Makes me nervous."

She shrugged and dumped the linen on the sofa. "In some areas I am trusting. In others, no." She would not give her heart again so easily, as she had with Lucian. Especially if there was a possibility that her money was the draw.

His gaze met hers for a long moment. Then he moved across the room, stopping right before her. Lightly, he touched her hair and softly flipped it behind her ear, sending chills up her spine. There were questions in his intense blues eyes, yet she had no experience deciphering what they truly meant. Cole was a man who masked his emotions well.

"Why did you cut your hair?"

How had they gone from trust to the length of her hair? She touched the shorter locks, felt the bubble of freedom, the same feeling she'd had six months ago when the hip-length tresses lay on the floor of the beauty salon.

"Are you one of those typical males who prefers long hair?"

"I didn't say that. The shorter length's nice. Pretty. I just wondered what prompted you to cut it off."

"Because it represented a fairy tale."

His brow rose, inviting clarification.

"Rapunzel. I dreamed of a knight in shining armor climbing the tower walls and saving me from the sheltered prison."

"Prison? Is that how you saw your life?"

His male scent surrounded her, tapping into long-ago images, hopes, dreams. Girlhood dreams that Cole would notice her, that he would be her savior knight.

Secret dreams that she'd finally given up on and unwisely transferred to Lucian—a terrible error in judgment.

"Sometimes." She stepped away before she gave into the urge to confess her youthful crush on him. He would think her a fool. Besides that, dreams changed. She no longer needed a knight—especially one whose life was anchored to a place and life-style she had no intention of returning to.

"Your family dotes on you."

"Oh, I know I am loved. It was the expectations that hemmed me in. From the cradle, I had to be so perfect. No blemishes that could possibly make me unsuitable to be a princess. There were so many classes in correctness. By the time I was a teen, I had no idea who I was anymore. I felt like a robot."

"Teens rarely know who they are."

"My circumstances were different. I saw a movie once, *The Stepford Wives*. Mama and I had gone to San Antonio to visit a friend. Mama's friend had a daughter my age and she had a television in her room." Her gaze turned inward, the vision so clear it could have been yesterday.

"Oh, I thought I was really getting away with something—to watch a show without first getting approval from my parents and instructors and anybody else who felt free to give input into the shaping of a princess."

She sank down on the sofa, curling her bare feet beneath her, hugging a pillow to her chest.

"I was horrified by that show because I saw myself there. Not as a beautiful princess who was cherished by her prince, but as a robot, like the Stepford Wives, trained to cater to a man's whims. Something happened then. I shrank into myself. And after that, whenever I saw Prince Joseph, I couldn't say two words to him. He represented a monster in my mind—one of those husbands of the Stepford Wives.''

His brow arched at her calling the crown prince a monster. "So you went in the opposite direction with Lucian?"

"We are all entitled to make mistakes," she said dryly, even though the punch of pain was still there.

"You're better off without the wimp."

She allowed a tiny smile at his sharp tone. "Lucian is an artist," she corrected.

"Still, he hurt you. I could track him down. Inflict a little pain."

She shook her head, touched despite herself. "I thank you for the gallant offer, but the wound is more to my pride. I thought I knew Lucian's heart and I did not. It has made me wary in the trust department."

"Not wary enough to keep your doors locked."

"That is a different type of trust." At his half smile, she shook her head and made a swipe at him with the pillow. "You are teasing me."

He dodged her playful missive. "You were becoming melancholy. You *do* need to take stricter precautions, though."

"Please do not use the word strict. I will balk on principle."

"Fine. *I'll* take the precautions."

Her shoulders lifted. "Suit yourself. Just do not cramp my style in the meantime."

"Woman, you are about as far from a subservient robot as a person can imagine."

"Absolutely. Now I am. And I intend to stay this way."

"Prince Joseph didn't know what he was missing."

Raquel laughed. "You have met Briana, no?"

"Yes."

"Then you know he is perfectly happy. She will love him as he needs to be loved. And she will keep him on his royal toes."

"You sound as if you know Briana well, yet how could you when you haven't been to the palace since the royal wedding?"

"We became acquainted *before* the wedding. Antonio and I went to the flower store in Antibes where Briana was employed. You see, when Joseph left in the middle of our betrothal ceremony, my father was certain we'd had a spat and insisted I locate the prince and make amends."

"I remember the trip," Cole said. "Antonio is as slippery as you when it comes to standing still for bodyguards. I was to accompany the two of you but was called away on another matter at the last minute."

Thank goodness, Raquel thought. At least with Antonio—the "spare heir" as he liked to call himself—she could be herself. Although Antonio was brother to the crown prince, he was a friend, confidant and surrogate brother to Raquel.

"Did you know Papa attempted to pay off Briana in order to clear the path for me?"

"Ouch." A muscle jerked in his jaw and his eyes softened in compassion. "I didn't think you knew about that."

"A mistake a lot of people made. Everyone was so busy trying to keep me in the dark. I allowed them to think that I had no interest in the goings-on around me. But I was very aware. Antonio is perhaps the only one who cared enough to look deeply...to notice that I was not an empty headed ornament."

"*I* noticed," he said dryly, a smile flirting with the corners of his lips. "It took a sharp, creative mind to skip the country without my immediate awareness."

"You know, Cole Martinez, I never realized you had a sense of humor. Can you keep a secret?" she asked abruptly.

"I do have the highest security clearance, spitfire."

"So you do. I had the aid of Queen Isabel."

He stared at her for several heartbeats. "You what?"

She nodded soberly, lips pressed together to hold back the grin. "My family still does not know."

"Well, I'll be damned. The queen spoke on your behalf when you disappeared, but she didn't mention she'd had a hand in the venture. There was quite a bit of chaos the day of the wedding when everyone expected *you* to walk down the aisle."

"I imagine there was. Actually, it was by accident that Joseph's mother and I were able to conspire. I had already left Valldoria, but before coming here, I stopped off to see Briana. That's where I literally ran into the queen. It seems we were both of the same mind as to who was the best princess for Joseph."

Cole prowled the living room, picking up several toys and tossing them into the playpen in the corner. For reasons he didn't dare examine, he was relieved to know Raquel wasn't harboring any secret feelings for Prince Joseph. Her feelings for the other prince, though, the one who denied his title, still nagged at him. He told himself he didn't care personally, that it was his job to cover all the bases.

Having picked up most of the mess that could cause a person to break his neck should he have to navigate the room quickly in an emergency, he turned back to

Raquel, leaning his elbow on the fireplace mantel, couching his words as casually as possible.

"Did Antonio know you were planning to skip town?"

"No. Once I made the decision, it was important that it be only *my* decision."

"Do you think he would have talked you out of it?"

She shrugged. "He would have played devil's advocate to be sure."

Cole hoped he didn't sound as much of an interrogator as he felt. "There was speculation that Antonio and you might have feelings—that you pined for him rather than Joseph."

Raquel laughed, the sound wrapping around him like a caress.

"Oh, no. Antonio is allergic to commitment. He has a love of all women and is much too wily to get caught by only one. Ours is more of a sibling-type relationship."

Cole was irritated with the relief he felt and made every effort to dismiss it. It did *not* matter that the beautiful, exotic heiress was emotionally free. He was only her glorified bodyguard. He told himself to remember that.

"Why haven't you come back home for a visit?"

"Knowing my papa you can ask me that?"

"He's not going to toss you in a dungeon."

"No but they still expect me to come to my senses, believing that my photography is only a passing fancy. I do not wish to fight, then leave again with a strain between us. As it is, our communications are fragile."

"And secretive. You've never once given your address."

She shrugged. "The fact that you are here tells me

that has never been necessary. I knew you would track me down. I am only surprised you did not come sooner.''

Cole rechecked the lock on the window. He could have told her he would have been here the very next day had he been commanded, but secretly he'd admired her grit in doing something so out of character.

The one thing that had almost made him jump the gun was when he'd found out Lucian had followed her to France. If the young artist had insinuated himself into Raquel's home, Cole would have been out here in a flash.

And there's where his information had gotten a little sketchy. He wasn't sure what had caused the separation between Raquel and her beau—he only knew he'd been more relieved than his position warranted.

It had taken some heavy negotiations, but he'd been successful in convincing Don Carlos to sit tight and let her try out her wings. The only stipulation had been that Cole keep tabs on her.

Which he had.

And as much as he wanted to deny it, some of those reasons *had* been personal. And intensely private.

MORNING SUNSHINE filtered through the open, lace-covered window. Tempting scents from the bakery next door permeated the room, mingling with the sweet smell of honeysuckle and geraniums that hung in a flower box outside her bedroom window.

Raquel stretched, smiling in anticipation of the babies that would come today for auditions. There could be as few as two or as many as fifty. No matter, each child would bring uniqueness to her photos with their precious expressions, whether in slumber or wide awake.

Tossing aside the sheet, she climbed out of bed, rubbing her eyes as she made her way to the bathroom. A glance in the beveled mirror above her dresser reminded her she hadn't removed yesterday's makeup. Mascara smudged the delicate skin beneath her eyes, giving her the look of a raccoon. The babies would think her a clown…or a monster. Best to set her appearance to rights so as not to startle anyone.

She frowned at the closed bathroom door. It wasn't like her to close doors—any doors. Even the cupboards in the kitchen suffered from the trait.

Twisting the knob, she pushed the bathroom door open.

And came to an eye-opening, wide-awake halt.

Cole Martinez stood at the sink, shaving cream covering his lower face. That was the only part of him that was covered, though.

The rest of him was as naked as the day he was born.

Piercing blue eyes connected with hers in the reflection of the mirror. The razor jerked. A sliver of blood welled.

Horrified that she had actually forgotten the man was in the house, she gasped. "*Madre de Dios!* Do not turn around!"

Chapter Four

Raquel's heart pounded like a drum. Shaken, she fled back across the hall to her room, slamming the door behind her. In this instance, a closed door was a must. She needed time to get ahold of herself.

She sat on the edge of the bed and covered her face with her hands. Not that it did much good. The image of Cole, *naked,* burned itself in her memory.

And she'd stared, for heaven's sake, stood there for what he surely would have noticed was an inappropriate amount of time. *Ogling* his attributes. Well, most of them.

She'd seen his tight, firm buttocks, his muscular back and his chest—compliments of the mirror's reflection. The porcelain pedestal sink had hidden his front unmentionables.

And for that small blessing, she would forever be thankful. Her fantasies were way out of hand when it came to Cole Martinez. She'd never seen a completely naked man—at least not in person. That her first experience had to be with Cole was unsettling to say the least.

How in the world would she face him?

A sharp rap on the door startled her right off the bed.

She shot to attention, a hand at her chest as if that would contain the wild beat of her heart.

Trembling, she waited to see if the bedroom door would swing open—and if he'd be dressed.

Obviously he practiced more restraint when it came to invading a person's privacy. Only his terse voice sounded through the closed door.

"The coast is clear."

She counted to twenty, then twenty again for good measure before peeking into the hallway. Finding the coast indeed clear, she darted into the bathroom, quietly closed the door and leaned against it.

Moist air surrounded her, fueling her fantasies all over again. The room smelled of Cole. Hot and musky, the essence of sex. *Male* sex.

Other than his scent, there was no other sign of him, she noticed. The room was spotless. All traces of water had been wiped from the sink, the fixtures and even the inside of the shower curtain. No wet towels hung in evidence of a bath—or graced the aqua tile floor, as was her habit. Her toiletries, which sat on the shelves above the commode, had been organized according to size and shape of each container.

Handy man, she thought. At home, there had been an army of maids to pick up after her. Accustomed to having things done for her, she'd never realized how sloppy and neglectful she actually was. Since acquiring a home of her own, the realization had become unimportant. So what if she didn't put things away immediately. She had only herself to please. If she happened to notice that the mess was becoming a tripping hazard, she eventually got around to picking it up.

There were just so many other things she considered more important. Like her photography. Already anticipating the day ahead of her, she stripped and hopped in the shower.

When she left the room a half hour later, lace panties were still on the floor, her gown lay draped half over the side of the hamper, the toothpaste cap was off, makeup pots were scattered about, and sprinkles of powder blush and eye shadows dotted the sink.

All the order Cole had restored had been unconsciously wrecked in a matter of minutes.

ONCE AGAIN the music was inappropriate in Cole's opinion. It conjured images of sex—not that he needed much incentive after the run-in in the bathroom this morning, with him stark naked and Raquel darn close to it.

He watched as her hips kept time with the beat of the music. She seemed to do it unconsciously. For a sheltered heiress, she'd certainly come out of her shell—in erotic glory, to his way of thinking.

And the clothes she wore, for crying out loud. He could see her bra plain as day! Black. Barely there. She wore a crochet thing that masqueraded as a top. Might as well have left the scrap in the closet. Sweat formed a damp line down his spine.

Por Dios! He would not last many days in this woman's company.

She looked around and spotted him. He tried to tell himself he hadn't been hiding…and knew he lied.

"Oh, Cole, come see."

He hesitated, feeling like a nervous cat surrounded by a pack of snarling pit bulls—which was a grossly exaggerated image, even for his suspicious mind.

A young mother held a blanket-covered infant in her arms. Both she and Raquel were gazing at the babe as if it were the Messiah Himself. He'd never been one to coo over a kid. Not because he hated babies or anything. It just had never occurred to him. He moved across the room and dutifully looked upon the newborn's face.

"Isn't he a love?" Raquel said. "So tiny and special. And but two weeks old."

Cole made what he hoped was an appropriate noise of appreciation. The kid slept peacefully in his mother's arms, never knowing the exotic dynamo touching his face so tenderly, camera hanging from a strap around her neck, was going to immortalize him in print, possibly even shape his life on the course to stardom.

"Yes, Mariana," Raquel said, her smile wide and happy. "Benjamin will do wonderfully."

Benjamin? Cole thought. Big name for such a little scrawny thing. The kid didn't even have eyebrows.

"I am in need of the small ones for the shoot," Raquel explained. She glanced at Cole, dragging him into the conversation, even though he wasn't particularly interested in being dragged there. He was too busy watching the door, wondering when the next person would waltz through without invitation, wondering if they would be friend or foe.

The lack of security here was inexcusable.

When Mariana and baby Benjamin left, the cottage was uncommonly silent. Cole didn't trust the lull. He was coming to learn that with Raquel, peace, quiet and orderliness were not part of her new persona.

The pessimist in him objected. Every operation needed guidelines, order, parameters in which to eliminate the possibility of missed clues. Missed danger.

"Is that the end of it?" he asked. They'd been coming in droves all day. Babies. Lots of them. Crying, smiling, sleeping, fidgeting. The place had been overrun with miniatures.

"I am not sure. But while there is a break in the baby auditions, I can work on the props."

The woman didn't stop moving, and he was forced to follow in her wake, trying desperately to keep his mind off the sexy sway of her jean-clad bottom.

"How can you call this an audition? You didn't turn away one single kid."

"Because they were all so perfect."

"They were all *alike*."

"Nonsense. Each had a wonderfully unique personality."

"How could you tell? Over half of them were sound asleep."

"I can tell."

He smiled at her resolute tone.

"You're good with the little ones." For the better part of the morning, he'd watched in admiration as she'd held them, soothed them, fallen in love with each little bundle. It was hard to believe she wasn't a mother herself. She had a knack for it.

"Thank you. They probably recognize a kindred spirit in me."

"How so?"

"Since I was surrounded by adults as a youth, I spent my quiet times in imagination."

"Rapunzel and knights, hmm?"

"That one was personal, and no longer so. Now the fairies are another matter," she said with an impish grin.

"Fairies?" he parroted. He did a lot of that around Raquel, he realized. Good thing none of his subordinates were present. He'd blow his tough guy image for sure.

"Of course. Can you not picture them coming out to dance in the raindrops?"

No, he couldn't. But he could imagine a child doing so. Not that there was anything childlike about the woman standing before him. Just the sight of her body was making him hot under the collar. Still, he realized that she interacted with babies so well because she shared their wonder at life. Of the universe.

9   But she also shared their naïveté, he decided, trying desperately to drag his mind back to business. Especially when he noticed that the door was again standing open, even though he'd shut it countless times that day.

"You need a security alarm," he announced, thinking aloud.

She frowned. "How did we go from fairies to alarms?"

"Did you forget why I'm here?"

Raquel shrugged. "I suppose I did."

The lifting of her shoulders drew his attention to her blouse—if it could even be called such a thing. His jaw clenched so hard it ached. "When did you start dressing so risqué?"

"I am having great difficulty keeping up with you, Cole." She glanced down at herself. "You call this risqué? In France? Besides, I am covered."

"Barely. I can see your bra."

"But not my breasts."

His back teeth were in serious danger of cracking. "It doesn't take much imagination to know their shape. They are half uncovered." He decided to shake the defiance he saw in her deep chocolate eyes. She could easily go overboard in her determination to live a carefree bohemian life-style. But if a person looked past the free-spirit veil, they'd see innocence.

And innocent lambs ought to know what would happen if there was a wolf in their midst.

Slowly, he reached out a single finger and traced the curve of her breast through the sheer top.

She drew in a breath, inadvertently pushing her chest more fully into his wandering touch. He could feel the pounding of her heart, see it in the pulse of her slender neck, and wondered if his own was as visible. His intention to shake her up had backfired. *He* was the one who felt unsteady.

Jerking back, he scowled and raked a hand through his dark hair. "More ground rules," he said tersely.

Her brow rose. "It is my home. Therefore the rules should be of my making."

"Not if you want to keep your virtue intact."

That sucked the wind out of her sails. But only for a second. It astounded him how quickly she could recover and dish it right back to him.

Her full lips, slick with a mauve-tinted gloss, pursed, reminding him that she wasn't the only one in the room with an active imagination.

"I am not worried over my virtue." Her voice, accented and sultry, curled around his gut and squeezed.

He was damned close to his limit, and scared spitless because of it. Stepping up to her, he crowded her, backing her against the wall. Arms bracketing her, palms flattened on the painted surface, he drew his knee up, pressing against her in a carnal way that got her immediate attention.

"Worry, spitfire," he warned softly.

Raquel could hardly draw a breath. Straddling his knee, she felt her body pulse in a manner that shocked her. Bravado was well and good, but it could get a girl in trouble. She stared into his fiery blue eyes, unable to look away. Her own palms were flat against the wall at her back. She didn't dare move.

No man had ever threatened her with such improper behavior. There was a dangerous slant to his eyes, a predatory, seductive glint that epitomized every fantasy ever raised about a Latin man.

A Latin lover.

And even though Cole was only half Latin, he did those countrymen proud.

A pulse beating at his temple told her he was a thread away from losing control. And that would be something to see, indeed. Cole Martinez did not lose control.

She probably ought to think twice about poking the beast this way. But something rebellious and highly curious egged her on...the curiosity over the seductive skill of a Latin lover.

She licked her lips, her gaze darting from the razor nick on his square jaw, then back to his fiery eyes. "What makes you so sure my virtue is intact?"

"Don't go there, Raquel." His voice was a gritty rasp, deep, dark and full of warning. And exquisitely thrilling.

"Why not?"

From knees to chest, their bodies pressed, sending a fire raging through her. Mesmerized, she wanted to explore that fire. With Cole.

She ran her palms over his unyielding chest, leaned into him. Music still drummed in the background, the beat becoming one with her pulse. His eyes softened, and she rejoiced that she just might have the power to tame this man who at one time had intimidated her so.

Their lips were a mere breath away from touching

before he seemed to get ahold of himself. He looked toward the ceiling as if seeking divine intervention, then whirled away from her, swearing—and doing a fine, highly inventive job of it.

"*Dios!* Not only do you disregard your personal safety, you…" He raked a hand through his hair. "This is unacceptable. I am going into the village to acquire an alarm system."

It was a minute before Raquel could clear her mind of the sensual haze. Did he intend to purchase a device to keep them apart? The notion of bells ringing should they get too close tickled her. And since Cole's very presence drew her like a magnet, the neighbors would get little rest if such a device existed.

And she really did need to rein in her overactive imagination. "For what?" she asked, masking her amusement.

"Your doors and windows."

"You mean like my family has at the estate?"

"I doubt that I can find anything so sophisticated. Still, simple is better than nothing."

"Not in my house. I do not have time to memorize codes and learn systems."

He glared at her. "Leave that to me."

"Cole, this is absurd. There are people in and out of here all day."

"And it needs to stop."

She frowned. "Do you not find it exhausting to be so suspicious?"

"If everybody had your Little-Red-Riding-Hood attitude, the world would be overrun with wolves."

She grinned. "Very good. Now you are getting into the spirit of fairy tales." She could have sworn he hissed.

"Don't try to sidetrack me, spitfire. You need an alarm, and I'm not in the mood to negotiate."

He had that stubborn look again, the one that told her he intended to have his way no matter what. Arguing would take time and no doubt be fruitless. Rather than continue the standoff, she shrugged and picked up a paintbrush to finish her set.

"Please yourself."

"As if I could," he muttered.

She smiled when the door closed with a snap behind him. The alarm project would keep him busy and happy. She'd just dismantle it when he returned to Valldoria.

The instant the thought surfaced, she felt a sharp stinging around the region of her heart.

She had no business entertaining sexual curiosity where Cole Martinez was concerned. Because he would be leaving, returning to his life and his work in the country of her birth. The country she no longer called home.

He was only in France because she was his current job, she reminded herself. And with that recall, came a punch of humiliation.

She'd practically thrown herself at the man.

Just like she'd jumped too quickly with Lucian. And look how *that* had turned out.

The hurtful memory straightened her spine and her resolve. Cole merely wanted her compliance. He was concerned over her safety until some deranged letter writer was apprehended.

Nothing more.

And despite her hard-won independence and her steady vows, despite her self-assurance over the success of her new life-style, it hurt that once again a man saw only an heiress when he looked at her. Just a woman who was *worth* something to him. A job in Cole's case.

Her heart pounded, washing the sting from her chest to the rest of her nerve endings. She'd learned that a woman could only be hurt if she allowed herself to care—and she'd sworn not to care about a man again.

Raquel was terribly afraid she'd already broken her own vow.

COLE CHECKED the wiring and modules again, then entered command codes into his laptop computer that would tie the whole alarm system together. It wasn't the best setup, but it would do.

Raquel had been cool with him for the past two days. He missed her spontaneous smile, her crazy talk of fairies, her wild ideas for new ways to capture the babies in print.

Hell, he even missed her messiness in the bathroom. She hadn't suddenly become the soul of orderliness, but she'd at least started picking up her scanty undergarments from the tile floor—which his blood pressure appreciated.

It seemed his health wasn't about to get a reprieve where Raquel Santiago was concerned, though. She'd left the house early this morning while he was in the shower. Either the woman was becoming a master at the art of giving him the slip or he was getting rusty.

Something he couldn't afford to do. The consequences could get ugly. Or somebody could end up dead.

He'd about decided to go hunt her down when he heard the sound of a motor.

He stepped outside and ducked beneath the archway on the patio, nearly having to fight his way through the spidery shoots of ivy. Raquel babied her flowers just like her human subjects, and it showed in the profusion of bright colors. The magenta petunias and trailing fuchsias were as clingy as the vines—and a hindrance to proper surveillance.

He didn't even want to suggest she cut the precious blooms, though. He counted himself lucky just getting the alarm installed.

He saw her coming up the cobbled street on a brown moped. Several doors away, she slowed the motorized bike as a group of young neighborhood boys flocked around her. One slick little Don Juan with round spectacles and a missing front tooth held out a bright-yellow marigold.

Obviously, the little boys in France learned their charm skills early. She laughed at their antics and took the time to chat with each one.

And Cole felt jealous of a bunch of little kids. He could barely drag his eyes away from her. She wore black patent sandals, tight hip-hugger pants and a sleeveless top tied beneath her breasts, showing a good portion of her middle. Sunglasses were pushed to the top of her head and a black handbag hung from the moped's handlebar.

Her fashion sense continually astonished him. And stirred his blood something fierce.

She looked up, then, and caught him staring. The smile faded from her lips. Damn it. What had he done to cause this frigid treatment? Pulled back instead of kissing her again?

He'd thought he was showing respect by not following through on his burning instincts to teach her a thing or two about the kind of relationship possible between a man and a woman.

The kind of relationship they could never have.

The moped, sounding like a well-tuned lawn mower, glided up next to him, nearly catching his toes. He noticed the sack of groceries strapped to the seat behind her. So, she'd been shopping. Still, clearing up the mystery of where she'd been didn't soothe his clamoring emotions.

"I wish you'd tell me when you intend to leave."

She shrugged, engaging the kickstand and gathering her purse and the sack. "I am out of the habit of announcing my every move. Do not attempt to imprison me."

"Damn it. I'm not..." He got a grip on his emotions. Barely. She brushed right by him. He almost forgot to duck and nearly smacked his head on the overhead archway. As it was, the killer vines snatched at his knit shirt.

Leaving a trail of leaves behind—another blight on his character, no doubt—he caught up with her, and plucked the grocery sack from her arms.

"I can manage."

"So you've said." He set the groceries on the kitchen counter and turned to her. They couldn't go on this way. It suddenly became important to him that she smile again. At him. Not just at the babies. Or at the neighborhood boys. Or at the countless *girlfriends* who streamed in and out of the house at will.

His instincts were to demand. He surprised himself by reaching out to softly touch her face. "Have I hurt you?"

She jolted at the intimate contact, her brown eyes going wide. "Why do you ask?"

He chastised her evasion with a gentle look.

Raquel sighed, stepping back before she was tempted

to lean into his tender caress. She dropped all pretense of indifference. It was exhausting to avoid him.

"You are a handsome man, Cole." Understatement of the year. "You make me think thoughts that are inappropriate for a short-term relationship such as ours. In an effort not to embarrass either one of us, I felt it wise to create some distance."

"You're very direct. A man could take advantage of that."

"But not you?" There was folly in dropping pretense. Thoughts slipped at will straight from her brain to her mouth without going through the censorship of propriety.

"Do not tempt me, Raquel."

"Could I?"

"Yes. I'm surprised you could even ask."

She shrugged, knowing she was on dangerous, untried ground. But a power she could not identify nor contain egged her on. "You are an expert at guarding your emotions."

"A lesson you seem to have forgotten."

"Not entirely. I do have my moments of remembrance, which is why I have been avoiding you. I am saving you the embarrassment should I lose my head and throw myself at you." Apparently her directness had left him speechless once again. She saw his hands fist, saw a muscle twitch at the corner of his eye, saw his chest expand as he finally drew in a deep breath.

"You haven't embarrassed me. I'm flattered, but... damn it, Raquel, I'm not the man you should be experimenting with."

"You would choose someone more like Lucian for me? An artist, perhaps?"

His jaw clenched. ''No. Someone more in your social class.''

''I am no longer in Valldoria. Here, I am in no specific class.''

''I won't be staying.''

Was it regret she saw in his blue eyes? She wasn't sure, but it gave her courage. ''I know, which actually could be to our advantage. No messy strings and recriminations to deal with as they say.''

He closed his eyes. ''We definitely need ground rules.''

''Give me a rule and I will undoubtedly break it.''

''But I won't.''

It amazed her that she actually thought she could push a man such as Cole. ''Good thing I do not wilt at rejection.''

''I'm not rejecting you, damn it. I'm protecting you.''

''Which is your forte.'' She turned and began unloading groceries, shoving them at will in the cupboards. ''You are off the hook, Cole. I will behave.''

''Forgive me if I don't trust that promise.''

She grinned and handed him a carton of eggs to put in the icebox. ''Okay, I will *try* to behave.''

''Will you go back to avoiding me?''

''I suspect, after this conversation, you will be the one doing the avoiding.''

''I can't. It's my job to be your shadow.''

''You certainly know how to puncture a girl's ego.'' His breath hissed out. ''That is not my intention.''

''Poor Cole. I am not what you expected, am I?''

''No. I wish...'' He didn't finish the sentence and Raquel's curiosity burned like a fire.

''What do you wish?''

He snatched at a cupboard and swore when it caught

on a childproof mechanism and slammed shut, nearly smashing his finger. With less force, he pulled again and depressed the latch. "That I could figure you out."

"I am an open book."

"You never used to be."

"People change."

In a very profound way, he thought. But he didn't want to pick up that particular conversational thread. He was barely treading water as it was. Much more of her directness and he'd go down for the count. Needing the diversion, he rearranged the canned goods, automatically turning them label out. "You'll let me know if you're leaving the house?"

"If I remember."

"Not good enough."

"When I am working I become scatterbrained. I will make the effort, though."

This was the hardest assignment he'd ever had. He'd seen her when she was wrapped up in her work. And she did forget things. Essential things, like eating. And if she could forget to eat, she'd surely forget to report her comings and goings, especially with the way she acted on thoughts as the impulse struck.

He'd have to stick closer. And that was damned well going to kill him.

Especially since she seemed determined to shake him up at every turn. Because if he wasn't mistaken, Raquel Santiago had it in her mind to do a little sexual experimentation.

Chapter Five

The triplets were the first to show up the next morning. They came in a stroller with three seats, sort of the stretch-limo model, Cole surmised. The mother appeared harried and distracted, talking with dramatic flair the minute she cleared the door.

The open door.

Good thing he hadn't yet rigged the alarm. Bells would be screaming.

"Oh, Raquel," she said. "I debated coming at all, but I am in a bind. My sister's husband, Louis, has suffered an accident and she is in need of comfort at the hospital. I know you need me to stay to help with the children...yet I cannot take them to the hospital with me—"

Raquel put her arms around the woman. "Do not give it another thought, Murial. You must of course go straight to the hospital and leave these babies with me." She tickled the chin of the child in the first seat. "We will get along famously."

Cole wasn't too sure of that. One person and three kids? Simple math told him there was a lack of available arms.

Before he could discreetly point that out, she'd shooed Murial out the door.

"Come to Tia Raquel," she said, lifting the babies out of the stroller, placing them in a playpen filled with toys.

Satisfied that she appeared to have things under control, he started to go back to his computer codes. The squeal of a baby and another female voice intruded.

"Ah, Tinisha, right on time. I see the costume fits Anthony nicely."

Anthony was obviously the baby—a little bigger than the other three. Anthony's mother—Tinisha—apparently intended to stay. Good. Two more capable arms. The math still didn't add up, but it was a given that women were pretty amazing at kid juggling.

With Tinisha's help, the triplets were outfitted with floral crowns in pastel shades and placed in individual baskets lined with soft fabric. And naturally, while the women's backs were turned, the curious kid in the bunny suit crawled over to a table and pulled himself up, pounding a plastic duck against the wood.

Since nobody was watching him, Cole felt honor-bound to keep his eyes peeled. From a distance. This wasn't his thing, and not having been exposed to them, kids made him jumpy. He was only interested in security. And safety.

He watched as Anthony bobbed in some sort of baby dance, causing the costume ears to flop. Cole grinned despite himself.

Then the grin vanished. The enterprising youngster let go of the table when no one was looking and toddled on unsteady legs toward a potted plant.

Cole's heart galloped as though he'd just been an

eyewitness to a crime in progress that was out of his jurisdiction.

Well, he was definitely out of his jurisdiction now.

The need for a split-second decision was at hand.

"Kid loose!" he shouted, feeling this was somewhat of an emergency. Acting on instinct, he took off at a run. Anthony gripped the fuzzy leaf of a newly sprouted African violet. Cole hooked an arm around the baby's belly and scooped him up. The plant went with them, scattering dirt all over the floor. "Drop it, kid."

The baby turned round eyes up to Cole and giggled.

"I guarantee you, that's no laughing matter. Tia Raquel is fussy about her plants."

Anthony ignored him and held out his prize.

"I warned you," he muttered as Raquel and Tinisha raced over.

The reprimand never materialized.

"Oh, you smart boy!" Tinisha exclaimed. "You walked."

Cole could have told them that. He handed the baby over to the excited mom, noticing a smudge of dirt on the white bunny suit.

"Oh, how wonderful that he has taken his first steps," Raquel said, obviously as pleased as if it had been her own child.

"He has taken several at a time, but never so many as to streak across the room this way."

Streak was right, Cole thought as he bent to wipe up the dirt from the hardwood floor. The little imp was a sure contender for the Olympic track team.

The two women continued to coo and praise. Finished cleaning up the mess, Cole stood and stepped back. He'd done his good Samaritan deed for the day.

That's when he noticed triplet number three crawling out of a basket—headfirst.

And by damn, nobody was watching. These pint-size troops needed a stricter sergeant at arms.

Swiftly, he changed direction, catching the infant just in time.

"No, no, sweetheart. Back in the basket you go." He assumed this one was a girl because of the pink wreath of flowers on her head. Gently, awkwardly, he tried to stuff the wiggly little girl back in her spot, but she reached her arms out, silently asking to be held.

Cole glanced around. Damn it, he hadn't signed on for this chaos. Criminals, he could handle. Babies were another matter entirely.

Raquel was behind the camera, taking a shot of the baby who'd impressed everybody with his first steps—and killed a plant in the process. *He* couldn't have gotten away with that. The leaves on the front patio he'd accidentally shredded yesterday had earned him a great deal of censure.

And that had been an accident. Anthony's act had been deliberate. He was losing it for sure. Reduced to competing with a child over the severity of a wrong.

He had more important matters to attend to. Like the gamboling triplets in front of him who were making him a nervous wreck—an emotion that felt totally alien.

Somebody needed to see to these kids. And it certainly wasn't his job.

"Uh, Raquel?" he called.

She barely glanced up from the camera. "Watch them for me, would you, Cole? I will be finished with Anthony in just a moment. Such a good boy you are," she cooed.

Cole's head whipped around. When he realized she was speaking to the baby, he felt foolish.

The adventurous triplet trying to escape the basket let out a shriek that got his attention. He sat down on the floor, guarding the three babies, feeling sweat trickle down his spine.

"What?" he asked, frowning at the baby.

She reached for him again. He put his hand on her puffed out tummy, surprised at how soft the skin was. When she poked out her lip and became more vocal he nearly lost what was left of his cool—which was very little. He felt conspicuous...and highly inadequate.

"Shhh, I have no idea what to do with you, but you're making me look bad." There was little choice but to lift her out of the basket.

Which appeared to be a mistake. Triplet number one thought that was some kind of signal. It stopped gumming the side of the basket, lifted its head and tried to wiggle out.

Headfirst again.

Hell, didn't these kids have any instincts for self-preservation?

With one arm wrapped around the baby in his lap, his other hand shot out to steady the escapee. "Sit," he ordered.

It plopped on its diaper-padded butt and hooked pudgy fingers in his watchband, tugging the metal into its mouth—never mind that his arm was still attached.

Warm drool dripped over his wrist.

He cringed but didn't dare move. At least the kid was staying put.

That is, until number two spied what its sibling had and wanted some, too. Their little heads butted as they each tried to get a slobbery mouth around his watch—thank God it was waterproof.

"Here, now. Don't fight." Neither one appeared to notice they'd knocked noggins. As gently as possible he extracted his arm and placed toys in front of number one and two, as he'd decided to call them. Wearing only a diaper and a soft crown of flowers, he couldn't determine gender. Not that he was an expert in doing that in the first place. Assigning sex according to the color of a flower wreath struck him as really thin reasoning.

The baby in his arms tugged at his hair and whimpered. He placed a palm at her diaper-clad bottom and felt the dampness seep into his shirt.

"Well, no wonder. You're soaking." And so was he, he realized with a fair amount of disgust. "Diaper change in basket three," he hollered.

The two remaining cherubs got tired of their toys and engaged in a curious shoving match. One smashed the other upside the head, causing a poked out lip and a frown. Cole might have laughed, but he was too far out of his element. He gently removed the pudgy hand from its sibling's ear, grousing that he was now reduced to being a referee.

Commanding the entire Royal Guard was a snap compared to corralling these wily kids. It was as if somebody had taken the lid off a basket of curious puppies. As fast as he got one back where it belonged, another one got loose. Or tried to, at least. Cole was doing his damnedest to be a good, kind, *gentle* warden.

And he was making a mess of it.

He was about to insist—strenuously—on reinforcements when a diaper appeared over his shoulder.

He looked up at Raquel, feeling like a man overboard without a life jacket. "You're kidding, right?"

She grinned and lifted the other kids out of the baskets. "I have two arms and two babies. We trade or you change the diaper."

"Where's the other woman? Surely she—"

"Tinisha and Anthony had to leave."

How had he missed that? Being aware of who went *out* the door as well as who came in was part of his job. It just went to show how rattled he was.

The challenge in Raquel's eyes made up his mind. How hard could it be to change a diaper? The television commercials he'd seen claimed the disposable variety came equipped with tapes.

He decided he was up to the task.

And revised that opinion several minutes later.

The little girl—he knew her gender for certain now—twisted and tried to crawl away. Sweat rolled down his temples. The baby let both him and the neighbors clear over in Nice know she had a magnificent set of lungs.

"What are you crying about?" he asked gruffly. "I'm the one in trouble here. You could have a little pity and make my job easier. I'm a beginner." The unhappy cherub stopped squirming.

Quickly he fastened the tapes on the diaper. It was crooked, but it would do. Before he could even pat himself on the back for what he considered an excellent feat, the kid started her gymnastics routine again, threatening to roll right off the changing table. He tried to keep her still.

Her voice grew louder and tears welled.

Oh, man. Not tears.

"Now, now. None of that." He picked her up and awkwardly patted her back. "I know I'm an amateur, but surely I didn't do too bad."

She rubbed her eyes and opened and closed her little fist.

"What?" When she continued her upside-down wave, he looked around. "Oh, the bottle. You're hungry? Well, why didn't you say so in the first place?" Man, it was hot in here. Once again, he looked around for reinforcements.

Raquel sat in a rocking chair, two babies, two bottles, two sets of sleepy eyes.

His sense of competitiveness reared. If she could handle two, he could deal with this one. He glanced down at the dark little eyes staring up at him, waiting for him to see to her needs. It scared the hell out of him. He didn't think he'd ever had anybody so dependent on him. She was cute as all get out, he admitted silently.

"If we're going to have a meal together, we should at least be on a first name basis, don't you think?" he asked, swiping the bottle off the counter.

"That's Alexandria," Raquel said softly.

He glanced up, feeling like an idiot. He'd forgotten she was in the room.

Forgetting was her trait, not his.

Raquel smiled and shook her head. "No sense pretending you weren't talking to the baby. Even macho guys like you cannot hold out against the charm of a little one such as Alexandria. She will wrap herself around your heart in seconds."

He shrugged and sat down in the unoccupied bentwood rocker. "I was only talking because it seemed to make her be quiet."

"But of course," she said, laughter dancing in her exotic brown eyes.

He couldn't hold her gaze. His image was blown and he felt out of control. Obviously there'd been a power shift—under these conditions, Raquel was the one with the experience. That gave her the upper hand.

Well, he prided himself on being a quick study. He'd get the hang of this baby thing soon enough.

"Looks like those two are asleep," he said, then glanced down as Alexandria wrapped her little hands around his on the bottle. He frowned. "Alex, on the other hand, looks like her eyeballs are about to pop out."

"Do not let her fool you. Babies can fall asleep within the blink of an eye."

"Hmm. Maybe your charges are just better behaved."

"Want to trade?"

"No thanks. It's become an important mission to see who comes out on top between me and little Alex here. So who are the well-behaved ones you're holding?"

"Antoinette and Annalisa."

"Why do all these little babies have such big names? And I was sure those two were boys. It would account for their manners."

"Do not attempt to make sexist remarks regarding these babies."

"Hey, *they're* the ones who got in a shoving match."

Raquel giggled. "Poor Cole. You did not anticipate this when you were sent by my father, did you?"

He didn't appear to hear her. His features were wreathed in awe as he stared down at Alexandria, who'd fallen asleep. Raquel smiled and carefully got up to lay Toni and Lisa in the crib. His question about big names had merit—especially when the parents shortened them to nicknames.

"You can put Alex in the playpen," Raquel said.

He nodded, but didn't get up. Raquel felt butterflies

take flight in her stomach. The sight of Cole gazing at the little girl in his arms gave her imagination a jump start—and heaven knows it was in full charge as it was.

Still, she could picture him holding his own child.

Their child.

And where that thought came from, she had no idea. As much as she loved the babies, she had no immediate plans to enter into motherhood. Added to that, she had no business picturing Cole and herself in such a union.

Hormones, she decided. They were becoming a nuisance. Probably the result of having bottled them up for twenty-five years.

She watched him lay Alexandria in the playpen.

"How long will they sleep?" he whispered.

"Anywhere from two minutes to two hours."

Cole actually tiptoed. "And when will Murial be back?" His respect for the triplets' mother grew.

"I do not know. But you have reminded me. I must send flowers to the hospital."

"You know her sister's husband?"

"No, but I know the sister. And it is the nice thing to do."

The correct thing, he thought. Watching her with the babies, barefoot, wearing an oversize shirt and capri-length leggings, he almost forgot she was a first-class heiress. She could choose place settings, converse with dignitaries and graciously serve tea to the queen. Polite manners were ingrained in her.

"Grab that bucket, will you?"

His brow lifted at her command. Maybe the manners weren't so ingrained. At least not with him. Nevertheless, he did her bidding and picked up the bucket.

"Where do you want it?"

"Next to the swimming pool."

"Swimming pool?" He looked around, and saw a plastic wading pool propped against the wall. Taking the initiative while she was on the phone ordering flowers, he rearranged the props, although he wasn't entirely sure what she had in mind.

The babies didn't nap more than half an hour. Antoinette, the physical one, seemed to be the instigator. She woke first and disturbed her bedmate. The activity disturbed Alexandria. Revived by the short nap, she sat up with a huge smile.

Cole figured since he'd sort of bonded with that triplet, he would handle her. He'd miscalculated, forgetting that Raquel needed to be behind the camera, and soon found out it was up to him to entertain and rearrange—all three of them.

Grumbling about the lack of hired help, he spent a hair-raising day carrying the kids around in the buckets—it was much easier than constantly lifting them in and out of the baskets and the handles were sturdy enough to bear the weight. When he wasn't toting the infants, he was shaking rattles and squeaking toys, trying to surprise just the right expression out of them so Raquel could get her shot.

They went through another round of bottles, and somebody—at this point he wasn't sure which one—spit up on him. He learned the art of shoveling baby food into a kid's mouth and ended up with mushy carrots decorating his already stained shirt. His shoulder was wet with drool, his back damp with sweat, and he swore he'd hand over his thirty-eight if someone would just let him lie down and take a five-minute nap.

Raquel, on the other hand, was as cool and calm as a gentle spring breeze. She took it all in stride, cooing, rocking and lulling the babies with an innate ease, as if she'd been around them all her life rather than sheltered in a fortress among adults who expected her to be poised and proper at all times. With both verve and patience, she snapped picture after picture, knowing just how long she could hold their attention.

Just watching her was a pleasure. Something gave way in Cole as she praised the babies, and then him when he impulsively stuck his tongue out, causing one of the triplets to mirror the gesture. Her laughter surrounded him, softening a heart he'd thought was tough as steel.

Since he'd spent his life pursuing his career, he hadn't given much thought to marriage or children. Yet he found himself picturing that institution now.

With Raquel.

A woman who far outclassed him.

Coming to his senses, he realized the longing was only a pipe dream, an isolated thought brought on by the wonder of these children—and the fascinating lady who captured their images so effortlessly.

She was only a job to him, he reminded himself. Her family paid his salary.

BY THE TIME MURIAL picked up the triplets, Cole felt as though he'd pulled a forty-eight-hour shift without sleep. The house looked like a cyclone had hit it. Even *he'd* been lax about picking up after himself.

He watched Raquel as she organized her cameras. That was the only area of her life in which she was meticulous about order. The urge to slip up behind her and sample the skin at her soft neck was almost overpowering.

And out of the question.

They hadn't actually verbalized any hard-and-fast

rules, but he had his own mental ones. And those included keeping his distance.

A sound at the door had him turning. Normally he would have jumped and whirled. He was getting too damned used to Raquel's life-style of people coming and going at will. And with the commotion of the babies, he'd forgotten all about connecting the alarm.

A woman hesitated just inside the doorway, a child cradled in her arms.

Raquel smiled and moved across the room.

"Bonjour," she said, the Latin accent rolling around the French pronunciation. "I am Raquel. And who have we here?"

Raquel lifted the fluffy pink blanket, softly touching the woman's shoulder at the same time. For some reason, there was timidness, or reluctance on the mother's part.

When she got a good look at the baby, she understood why.

"I am Claudia." The woman hesitated. "This is my daughter, Hope...." Her next words were delivered in a rush. "She is a Down's syndrome baby, and she might not be right for your project, but I saw your ad for auditions and I couldn't make it on the day because of doctor appointments, but I thought...well, if she's not what you're looking for, I'll understand."

"Oh, she is indeed a blessing," Raquel said softly, looking right past the handicap to the beauty of the child. "Look at those precious eyes." She held out her arms. "May I?" She liked to hold the children, to make sure there was a rapport, a bonding. If a child hated her on sight the shoot would not go well. So far that had never happened.

Claudia nodded, relief and gratitude in her eyes. And pride.

Raquel accepted the child, pressing her lips to a sweetly rounded cheek. She could not begin to imagine the demands of caring for a handicapped child, nor the torment a mother must suffer over the stares, pity and thoughtless questions an uneducated public would most likely level at them. Her admiration for Claudia's courage in bringing Hope was immense.

"How old is she?"

"Sixteen months."

Raquel didn't bat an eye, even though the baby was no bigger than a six-month-old. Cornflower-blue, wide-spaced eyes stared up at her. Despite the slightly irregular features, Hope appeared just like any other baby. Soft, warm, uniquely special, smelling of baby talc and formula. Rosy lips widened into a precious smile and Raquel's heart turned over. She could already imagine the finished poster, with the child's name in big letters across the bottom.

Hope. The name, the single word, said so much.

"May I photograph her now?"

"Are you sure? I don't expect...I had only come about the audition."

"She is beautiful, Claudia. And I mean that from my heart." Clearly, Claudia was concerned that Raquel was speaking out of pity. Nothing could be farther from the truth.

"Thank you."

"It is I who will be thanking *you* when we see the finished product. I must ask, though, how is she in water?"

"She loves her bath time."

"Oh, this is the perfect day. So many of the babies

do not like to get wet. I have been waiting for an opportunity to try a shot in the wading pool.''

"She doesn't sit up on her own," Claudia said, her gaze clinging to her little daughter as if she was used to making excuses, yet fiercely protective in the process.

"That will not be a problem. We will surround her in a cocoon of cotton batting. There will only be a few inches of warm water, so do not fear she will topple over. My assistant will watch her very closely."

She turned. "Cole? Will you ready the pool? Use extra cotton, curved around the lip of the pool rather than the middle," she instructed. "That way we will assure support."

Cole nodded and automatically set to the task. He was getting used to the way she issued orders. Bossiness aside, though, he found that he liked the way she included him, relied on him even.

As he dragged the pool into position, he listened and watched as Raquel bonded with her newest modeling subject, both awed and humbled by the way she treated the child as if she were perfect.

He thought of all the times he'd judged someone because of a weakness, telling himself that only the strongest, most physically fit would do for his military. He'd been rigid, choosing to bypass those with flaws rather than give them a chance.

"Such a pretty little girl you are," Raquel cooed. Cole could barely keep his mind on his task. His admiration for Raquel's professionalism and compassion was so great he wasn't sure how to compartmentalize it. And it somehow seemed important that he do just that. Otherwise, this host of new, untried emotions might crumble his solid foundation.

Holding the child, she walked over to the stereo and selected some music, something soft, soothing, her expressive chocolate eyes gauging the baby in her arms.

"Yes," she pronounced softly to Hope. "Feel-good music. You like that, don't you?" She swayed to the easy notes. "I think we will snap a few dry photos, just in case you do not like my fun bathtub. We must not miss the opportunity to make you a star."

Professional, smart and a hell of a woman, Cole thought.

Cole hooked a hose to the sink, tested the water temperature and filled the plastic kiddie pool with the required inches. Across the room, Raquel snapped picture after picture, the camera's strobe light flashing.

It amazed him how quickly she could get her pose, coaxing really cute expressions from the kids.

He stood when she came over to him. Hope was now outfitted with little feather wings resting atop her shoulders.

"Do you want the headpiece?" he asked, his deep voice drawing the attention of the child.

"No," Raquel said. "I do not want to draw away from her wondrous expression."

"You're right."

She glanced at him, her eyes soft and shining with appreciation. He felt uncomfortable.

Well, hell. Handicapped or not, the baby was a cutie.

"You are a big fraud, Cole Martinez." Before he could ask for clarification of that remark, she turned her attention back to Hope. "And you are a natural at baby modeling, aren't you, *ma chérie?*"

She tested the water temperature and lowered the wide-eyed little girl into the nest of fluffy cotton.

Hope tentatively touched the water.

So far so good, Cole thought. No ear-piercing screams.

"She will do fine," Raquel said. "Stay close."

Quickly, professionally, she raced behind the tripod and snapped photos, laughing, singing, praising. The little girl beamed and waved her arms, her tiny hand landing with a slap against the surface of the water.

The splash startled her. Wide-set eyes became even more round. Cole automatically inched closer, waiting for the baby to scream. Instead, she let out a squeal, her open-mouth grin bringing a lump the size of a bowling ball to his throat.

Where had that emotion come from? He wasn't one to get choked up over babies. Claudia stood off to the side, her hands folded and pressed against her mouth, her lips trembling with pride and joy.

He glanced at Raquel, saw moisture spill over onto her cheeks. She never stopped snapping pictures, nor did she wipe away the signs of soul-stirring sentiment.

For a woman who'd once been an expert at appearing emotionless, she'd done a complete about-face. There was nothing uppity about her, no indication that she was one of the richest women in the world who normally attended charity functions in priceless gowns and wore expressions of poised subservience. Or disinterest.

The emerging facets of this woman continually intrigued and amazed him.

Raquel at last lowered the camera and nodded.

"Finished?" he asked softly.

"Yes."

He was the closest, having stayed just outside the area of frame in case a steadying hand was needed. Carefully, he reached in and lifted the wet little girl, transferring her to Raquel's arms and the towel she held waiting. Their fingers brushed as they each steadied the baby.

Their gazes met and held for what seemed an eternity. He reached out and swept a thumb beneath her eye, wiping away the moisture.

"You are something else," he said softly.

"As are you."

If he'd allowed himself to imagine the type of woman he'd choose as a mate, Raquel Santiago would fit. If they weren't coming from two different worlds, he could easily picture himself moving heaven and earth to have her. To hold her. To call her his own.

And the impossibility of that image twisted in his gut like a white-hot dagger.

Chapter Six

Two hours later, Raquel rushed out of the darkroom, a folder of newly developed prints in her hand. The images she'd captured were priceless, especially the ones of Hope. Her immediate, unconscious mission was to find Cole, to show him the fruits of their combined efforts.

Excitement bubbled within her. She'd never had anyone to share this part of her day before.

Halfway through the living room, her steps slowed. She shouldn't be pinning hopes and warm feelings of new experiences on Cole. He was only a temporary part of her life, a visitor with a purpose that had nothing to do with quiet evenings of sharing, touching and encouraging.

Tracing the edge of the folder, she waged a silent debate, then set the photos on the coffee table.

The smell of food permeated her confused senses and her stomach rumbled. The scent wasn't from the bakery next door. It was closer and even more tempting.

She paused at the kitchen doorway. Cole stood at the stove, stirring something in a pot. He wore a flowered apron—where he'd found it, she had no idea. She didn't recall ever seeing that particular article of clothing. Not that she'd have paid much attention. Her trips to the kitchen were on a need-to basis, and usually didn't involve anything more messy than popping something in the microwave.

A smile touched her lips. The blue peonies trimmed in lace should have looked feminine. On Cole, it looked just the opposite.

He was so confident in his masculinity, he could have worn a baby bonnet and made it look macho.

Candles burned in the center of the small table draped with an ecru linen cloth. Garden salads were prepared and sitting on mismatched ceramic plates.

Her heart fluttered. After a day of watching those large, capable hands cradle small babies, of seeing the amusement and enjoyment he hid behind gruffness, she'd felt her emotions slipping in a direction they had no business going in.

She'd vowed not to give her heart to another man. Seeing him in her kitchen, preparing a meal for her, was the final matchstick that tumbled the fortress. Her heart pounded in both dread and anticipation as a wildfire of conflict raced through her system. Terror over the revelation nearly buckled her knees.

Because as much as she'd promised herself otherwise, Raquel had fallen in love.

It was the most exciting, terrifying, potentially heartbreaking thing she could have done.

Gathering her composure, she stepped into the kitchen, doing her level best to act normal.

"I am impressed."

He looked around and frowned, staring at her for a long, heart-stopping moment. *Madre de Dios!* Did he see with his eyes what she had only moments ago realized? That would be a disaster. Even if it came to sharing herself with this man, she would not share those words. They would only create pain when the time came for them to part.

And they would part eventually, she reminded herself.

She lifted her chin, drew on the natural instincts she'd buried when she'd come to France, allowing her gaze to appear uninterested—the empty-headed heiress look, Antonio had teased on more than one occasion.

Cole's frown deepened, but at last he looked away. "Sit. Chicken's done." He pulled a casserole dish out of the oven. "The temperature's off on this stove. It cooks hot."

She sat at the table and snitched a roll from a covered basket. Had he actually gone next door for the bread? That would have been brave and enterprising on his part. "I would not know. I rarely use it."

"Humph. You rarely eat, as far as I can tell. You need somebody to take care of you."

"I do fine." His gruff statement endeared him to her rather than raised her defenses. "What possessed you to cook? When I went into the darkroom, you looked ready to collapse."

"I figured if anybody was going to get a meal around here, it would be up to me to cook it."

"We could have gone out."

"It wouldn't look very good if I fell asleep over my dinner plate in public." He poured steaming vegetables into a serving bowl. "How do you do it? You don't look the least bit tired."

"The babies are exhausting, yes, but they also energize me. And when I see the developed prints, the excitement revives me."

"I could use you in my Guard. You'd run circles around some of my soldiers."

He placed the casserole dish in front of her. The whole atmosphere impressed her—the food, the formality of the table setting, the candles. He'd gone to a great deal of trouble and hadn't neglected a single detail.

In her country, the women were taught to cater to the men—a trait she had shed immediately upon coming to France, vowing never again to bow to a man's whims.

Still, in her old life, it would have been up to her to see to a meal. Even if she didn't cook it herself, she would be expected to organize it.

Now, here was Cole. Catering to her. Her bathroom gleamed, toys were picked up and stored in the toy chest, dirty dishes were put in the dishwasher rather than sitting in the sink, and now…dinner.

Served by a sexy man in a flowered apron.

Talk about a fantasy. She rather liked the role reversal.

"You surprise me. Latin men are normally reluctant to share what they consider women's duties."

"Guess my American heritage is showing. My mother insisted this was a custom every boy should learn. No gender boundaries in our household."

"Really? And your father, he did these women's chores also?"

"Cooking's not a woman's chore."

Her brows arched at his look of affront. "My apologies. I lost my head for a moment. Princess training, you understand."

"I doubt a princess spends time in the kitchen." He removed the apron and sat down across from her.

She hid a smile. He had baby spit up on his shirt and

smudges of paint from the props. He needn't have bothered with the additional protection from stains. But that was Cole, she realized. Ever organized, all his ducks in a row, follow the rules by the book. Somebody had probably once told him the rules said he had to wear an apron.

"You are right, actually. Other than conferring with the staff, I rarely entered the kitchen. Didn't you have staff at home?"

"No."

"Then did your papa cook?"

His lips quirked. "Yes. But he threatened us with a firing squad if we told. He was pure-blood Latin."

"And very much in love with your mother to do for her in such a manner."

"He idolized her."

She savored a bite of spicy chicken, noticing the sadness that crept into his vivid blue eyes. "I remember him, you know." Raul Martinez had been head of the Royal Guard before Cole, before an early heart attack had taken his life and Cole had stepped into his position. "He was a good man."

"The best. There hasn't been a day for the past five years that I haven't missed him like crazy."

She reached out and touched his hand. "He would have been proud of you."

He shrugged. "He was a good teacher."

"You trained under him? I do not recall seeing you."

"There was no reason for our paths to cross then. Actually, I received my military training in the States—counterintelligence and weaponry."

"And I am certain you excelled at it."

"I liked my job."

So modest, she thought. A lot of men would have

jumped on the opportunity to boast. But not Cole. She had an idea he had plenty of commendations that would attest to his capability. Aside from that, his self-assured carriage and the fact that her father and the king trusted him completely spoke volumes about his competence and skill.

"What made you go back home?"

"Mother called and mentioned that Dad was slowing down, appearing more tired than usual. I quit and came home."

"Just like that?"

"It was family."

She checked his tone for censure, wondering if he was subtly suggesting that she should have done the same at the first hint of unrest surrounding her own father. She pushed her fork around on her plate, separating grains of rice from the chicken.

He reached out as if to touch her hand, then pulled back. "I wasn't judging you, Raquel."

She met his intense gaze. "Did they teach you mind reading in your counterintelligence course?"

"It doesn't take a clairvoyant to read you. At least not anymore."

"As opposed to…?"

"When you were preparing to become the princess, you were an expert at holding your cards close to your chest."

"Where now I play them face up?"

"Most of the time."

"I shall have to try for more mystery. I understand men like that."

His hand jerked, and his eyes narrowed. "In my business, mystery usually means danger. I prefer openness."

He knew the minute he said the words he was in trouble. Those exotic brown eyes sharpened.

"Oh, good. I dislike games. If I am easy to read, we will not misunderstand one another."

"Raquel," he warned, knowing exactly where she was going with this line of reasoning. He saw curiosity and determination. He'd suspected Raquel intended to turn up the sexual heat and make his life hell. He was equally determined to head her off at the pass.

"Do not worry, Cole. I know you are tired tonight."

He snatched up his plate and nearly toppled over the chair as he stood and headed for the sink. This woman spelled danger with a capital D. And if he didn't get away from her he was going to do something incredibly stupid. Like take her in his arms and kiss her, to give her exactly what she was asking for and more.

"It has nothing to do with being tired."

Raquel smiled when she saw him tug at his collar. Good. He'd been playing havoc with her libido since the moment he'd crossed the threshold, insisting on dragging her back home.

But deeper than the physical was the respect she felt for him, his tender confusion with the babies, his indulgence of her whims, his dedication to his country and her father...and to her. There were so many layers to this man that he hid behind a mask of duty. And she wanted to uncover each facet, experience them all.

Including intimacy.

Her virginity was the one thing she had yet to give up—she'd emerged in every other aspect of her life except this one. And even knowing they had no future together, it had become increasingly important to her that Cole be the man to teach her about the physical side of love.

However, at the moment he looked ready to bolt, so she decided to give him a break. "Thank you for helping with the babies."

The relief that crossed his features at the subject change was almost comical. "No problem. Ever thought about hiring an assistant?"

"No. So far, this is the largest project I have taken on. And usually the parents help out—with the babies only, though. I do not ask them to muscle around the props, which is why I am grateful for your help with the pool. Otherwise it would have been necessary to reschedule Hope's session."

"I think you managed to get some good material." Cole leaned against the counter, determined to stay right there—six feet away from her. He felt like a coward, but damn it, this woman was too tempting for his peace of mind.

"Oh, I did." Her eyes lit with excitement. She stood, reached for his hand and pulled him along behind her. "I have processed the film. You must see."

The strength in her soft hand took him by surprise, as did her abrupt actions. His first instinct was to snatch back his hand, but he couldn't bring himself to dampen her enthusiasm.

As long as her mission was aimed at photography and not him, he felt safer. Which was probably a mistake. This dynamo had a way of keeping him off balance and on his toes.

She picked up a folder from the coffee table and tugged him down beside her on the sofa. Her wildflower scent tantalized him, the heat from her bare arm raising his blood pressure. He started to scoot over, to create distance.

His ploy failed. She scooted right along with him.

He glanced at her sharply, but she was busy arranging glossies. Although the move appeared to be unconscious, he didn't trust that innocence.

She flipped her hair behind her ear and reverently touched a photo.

Cole's gaze skimmed the smooth skin of her arm, down to where her slender fingers rested against an eight-by-ten photo. He could no more stop the gentle smile that curved his lips than he could stop the sun from rising in the east.

Baby Hope sat in the pool, tiny feather wings resting atop her bare shoulders, a wide-eyed look of wonder in her bright-blue eyes as she looked upward as if she were gazing upon the face of an unseen angel. He remembered the expression—only a split second, actually—when she'd splashed the water. She'd gone from startled to amazed to laughing.

Raquel had captured the best of all three.

The caliber of her talent could not be disputed.

"Amazing," he said softly.

"She is," Raquel said, gazing at the photo. Her eyes said so much. "I will enlarge this one and put a single caption beneath. Just her name. *Hope.*"

"This photo alone will cement your future as an artist."

"It will sell well, perhaps gain me name recognition. As for monetary, any proceeds from this one will be donated to benefit Down's syndrome children."

"You have a heart as big as the Mediterranean."

"Hope is the one with the heart," she dismissed. "And Claudia. It took great courage to bring her daughter today."

"She was lucky. She chose the right photographer to bring her to. Let me see the rest."

He chuckled at the picture of Antoinette shoving Annalisa. "Sibling rivalry?"

"Hmm, it has possibilities. Or sisterly love perhaps?"

"Looks more like war to me."

"That is because you are a pessimist."

He shrugged, knew the characterization fit and flipped through the photos. There was a shot of Lisa chewing the lip of her basket and one of Alex with her pudgy arms reaching toward the sky. The next showed all three babies in a group hug with one stuffed rabbit. Then the triplets—side by side in their baskets—Alex sticking out her tongue, Toni frowning at her sister's lack of manners and Lisa once again gumming the basket, unconcerned with her siblings' antics. "Cute one," he said.

Raquel shifted closer, her hand on his thigh.

He went very still. Her fingers burned through his jeans, making his thoughts shoot straight from babies to adult-only images.

She gave his leg a squeeze. His head whipped around, but she leaned forward to straighten the glossies.

He frowned. Had he been mistaken about the pressure? Get it together, man, he lectured silently, flipping to the next photo.

Not a baby shot this time. Just him. Alone. The barest hint of a smile on his face as he'd watched Alex sleep. He hadn't realized she'd photographed him. And why had she? Although he knew it shouldn't, it somehow pleased him. Personal rules aside, it gave his ego a boost to know that she thought of him, that she watched him, that she was interested enough to snap a covert picture.

He heard her indrawn breath.

"Oh, I forgot about that one." She made a grab for

it, but he held it away. "I was merely testing the camera and the shutter clicked accidentally. I thought there was no more film and—"

"Raquel?"

"What?"

"You are a terrible liar."

Her brow arched.

"An accidental shot wouldn't be in perfect focus. And you obviously discovered there was additional film when you went to all the trouble to process the print."

She leaned into him again, her soft breast pressing intimately against his arm. Her hand curved over his on the print as she angled it toward her. "It is a good picture of you."

He turned his head at the same time that she did. Her lips were so close. Her floral scent wrapped around him, tormented him. Like a freeze-frame, time stood still, the air shimmering with intangible waves of electricity. Silence stretched, broken only by the tick of the mantel clock, a steady cadence that seemed to explode with each advancing second, taunting, urging, *insisting*.

He saw her eyes widen, then soften with anticipation, asking questions he had no business wanting to answer. A smart man would resist that invitation.

And he prided himself on having a fair amount of intelligence.

But before he could exercise good judgment, she took the matter right out of his hands and pressed forward, touching her lips to his. Soft. Man, she was soft. And sweet.

His heart pounded against his ribs. Just for a minute, he promised himself. Then he would be strong and pull back.

Her tongue touched the seam of his lips, setting off

an explosion of heat. The tentative exploration nearly did him in. She was too much for a man to resist.

The photo fell from his fingers as he cupped her face, angling her head for better access to that sweet, sassy mouth. He pulled her to him, feeling her breasts pillow against his chest. His body's reaction was both incendiary and painful within the restriction of his jeans.

He kissed her the way he'd longed to kiss her for more years than he cared to remember. Savored, explored, torturing himself with this brief taste of the forbidden.

Her surprisingly strong fingers dug into his shoulders, shooting his desire straight up and over the top. He ached to lay her down on the sofa, cover her body, push her legs apart and bury himself inside her warmth.

Only he couldn't. It would be a betrayal to her family and his trusted position if he were to give in to this burning attraction. This need.

Although his instincts screamed at him to jump up and run as fast and as far as he could, he surprised himself by pressing his lips to her forehead. He could feel the beat of her pulse, hear the escalating strength of her arousal in her soft moans and rapid breathing.

Watching her come alive in his arms was sweet torture. He almost wished she'd go back to her haughty heiress persona, hiding her emotions behind a mask of indifference. Because this new woman was deadly to a man's good intentions. Her chocolate eyes were full of erotic questions that were all the more irresistible because of their innocence.

And he'd made up his mind right off that he would *not* be the man to answer those questions, to satisfy that curiosity that begged to be appeased.

Frustration rasped in the back of his throat as she

unconsciously flowed against him, nearly climbing into his lap. It took every ounce of control he possessed to gently hold her back.

Her gaze was unfocused as she looked at him. "Why did you stop?"

"I should have never started in the first place." Actually, *she* had been the instigator.

"Why?" The bewildered look of innocence contrasted with the flush of sensuality on her cheeks, the heaviness of desire in her dark eyes, the thrust of her nipples visible through the stretchy tank top she wore.

Hell on fire, he had to get out of here. Fast.

He stood. "You're way too good for someone like me, Raquel." And with that, he headed across the room, ripped open the front door and strode into the night.

Raquel stared at the closed door. She didn't know what to do with the wild desire coursing through her body. She had no experience with these sensations. Her skin felt tight and tingly, her lips swollen. With each beat of her rapid pulse, a decadent throb pulsed in her femininity.

Obviously she was doing something wrong, but she had no idea what.

That's when she remembered her girlfriends. This was France, not Valldoria where she had to suffer alone, where she had to worry over convention or status or making a wrong step before the watchful eyes of an entire country.

Yes, she decided, one of those wonderful chats with Sasha and Margo was definitely in order.

After all, she hadn't jilted a royal prince and run off to strike out on her own without learning a thing or two about herself—like her dogged determination.

ALTHOUGH IT WAS LATE, Cole put in a call to Johnny Cruz. He was confident of Cruz's abilities to handle both the investigation and the Guard. Still, he wanted an update. Wished the whole hint of unrest was over and done with.

The sooner he got back to Valldoria, away from the temptation of Raquel, the better off he'd be.

The line connected halfway through the first ring.

"Cruz, here."

"Anything new?" Cole asked.

"Quiet. I'm beginning to think the threat was a hoax."

"Yeah, and thoughts like that can land us among the ranks of the unemployed. I'm fairly partial to eating myself."

"I hear you, man." Cruz chuckled, if it could even be called that. The second in command was more stingy with his emotions than Cole himself was. "I'm still checking on Cordoba and Patillas. No sign yet of the money Cordoba stole, but I'll find it. In the meantime, the guy's threatening lawsuits over the loss of his job."

"Figures. Gets caught with his hand in the cookie jar and blames somebody else. Any leads on him being behind the warning letter?"

"Nothing so far. Either the guy's innocent—as he claims—or he's slippery as hell. How about your end? Any moves on the heiress?"

Cole's heart lurched. It took him a moment to realize Cruz wasn't referring to the moves *he* ached to put on her. Dangerous moves that had nothing to do with investigative procedures.

"No," he finally said.

"How much longer will you stay?"

"Hard to say. I suppose until Santiago orders me

back, or Raquel gives in and comes home." He'd already given Cruz a thumbnail sketch of Raquel's professional obligations, leaving out the personal reasons she balked at returning to Valldoria. "I'll be able to make a better judgment once we get the info on Cordoba and Patillas."

"And Phil Domingez," Cruz inserted. "Forklift driver at the shipyard. Cordoba insists Domingez is our man."

Cole wrote down the name and pertinent details. "I'll see what I can come up with on this end. Any of them mention Miss Santiago?"

"Only in the sense of knowing *of* her. Which doesn't mean squat. *Everyone* knows of her."

Yeah, and Cole in particular wanted to know a *lot* more. "Okay. Keep at it. I'll be in touch."

WITH NO BABIES scheduled for the morning and Cole busy fiddling with his laptop computer, Raquel decided it was a good time to slip next door to the bakery. She started to walk out, then hesitated. She wouldn't put it past him to tear apart the village looking for her.

Reporting her whereabouts chafed, but in the interest of harmony she compromised and tacked a hasty note to the doorjamb—right next to the ridiculous alarm box Cole insisted on activating.

The cramped kitchen of St-Pierre's bakery sweltered from the heat of industrial-size ovens, the air redolent with the mingling scents of fresh-baked breads and pastries.

Sure of her welcome, Raquel entered through the alleyway door.

"Well, hello stranger," Sasha said, slipping her

hands into oven mitts. "Are you here to schedule Carmen for a photo shoot?"

No, that wasn't her purpose, but it was a good starting point. She needed to ease into this delicate conversation. "Partly," she said. "I could use her this afternoon if you would like time for yourself."

"I do have some errands to run. But won't you need me to help?"

"Cole can assist me."

"Ah, the sexy houseguest who is causing you to neglect your friends."

Raquel's eyes widened. "Oh, Sasha, I have upset you."

"No, you haven't, silly. I was teasing."

"Oh." Unused to having close friends, she was always afraid she'd do something wrong. There were times when she had to sit on her hands to keep from calling too often. She did not want to monopolize or be a pest. But Sasha and Margo never gave the impression that she demanded too much of their time. They were always more than willing to put on a pot of coffee and take a break.

Since Cole's arrival, they'd fallen behind on their get-togethers. And with what Raquel had in mind, she suspected the visits could very well become even more infrequent—at least for the duration of Cole's stay.

No, she decided. She would not let that happen. Surely she could balance the two relationships. Especially with the lack of success she appeared to be having with Cole.

"Actually, I have come to ask a question."

"*Oui?*" Sasha invited.

"I would like to know how to seduce a man."

Sasha lost her hold on the breadboard she'd just removed from the oven. Quick reflexes saved the fluffy croissants before they ended up in the sink. She put the rolls on a rack to cool and turned, her blond brows nearly disappearing beneath fluffy bangs.

"You certainly know how to drop a conversational bombshell. Are we speaking about any man in particular? Or shall I alert the local men that their dreams are about to come true?"

Raquel rolled her eyes. "Do not make this difficult, Sasha. I have always been able to count on you to be frank with me."

Sasha poured them each a cup of coffee and joined Raquel at the table. "Assuming we've set our sights on a man who's conveniently under our roof...?" Her words trailed off until Raquel nodded. "Well then, the direct approach is always a good starting point."

"That's the problem. I don't know direct from indirect."

"Conversation, sweetie," Sasha clarified. "Come right out and proposition the man."

Raquel sucked in a breath. "I could not do that!"

"Girl, where have you been? In a convent?"

"Close. Educate me, Sasha—with a mind toward subtlety. I do not want to clobber the man over the head with my intentions."

"I am not known for subtlety. And you don't need education. Unless the man is blind. Your exotic eyes alone would seduce."

"It's not working."

"Are you sure you want it to?" There was concern in Sasha's eyes.

"Yes. It is time, Sasha. My reasons are...well, I am shedding the trappings of my old life."

"Sometime you will have to tell me of this life."

"Yes, but that would take us off the subject," she evaded.

"Okay, let me think. Do you have a tattoo?"

"No!"

"Pity, you could offer to show and tell."

"I'm talking subtle, here. Not brazen." She couldn't stand the curiosity. "Do you have one?"

"Yes."

"No!" Never would she have guessed this about sweet, motherly Sasha. With her bouncing blond hair and ready smile, the woman was as down-to-earth as they came. "May I see?" As the sound of her request registered, she let out a peal of laughter. "Not that I am practicing seduction on you, you understand."

Sasha's eyes twinkled as she stood and gathered up the hem of her flowing sundress, exposing her upper thigh. Raquel inspected the small rose discreetly positioned so it would only be visible in a skimpy bathing suit…or if unclothed in the privacy of a bedroom.

"Oh, it is beautiful, and delicate…and very daring of you to have done such a thing. How long have you had it?"

"Since before I married Paul."

Raquel's brows arched. "And did you use it as a seduction technique?"

"Absolutely. I told him about it…teased his imagination."

"Then you showed it to him," she guessed, trying to imagine the expression on conservative, straight-laced Paul St-Pierre's face.

"No. I made him find it."

Raquel nearly choked on a sip of coffee. "You are bad! However, since I have nothing to show off, what is your next suggestion?"

"Well, there is always licking the lips."

"Why?"

Sasha sputtered a shout of laughter. "Oh, I see it will be necessary to start from scratch with you. We must get Margo in here to aid the lessons, I think."

"Did I hear someone call my name?" Margo paused in the kitchen doorway. With a black spandex top stretched over her ample breasts and long carrot-red hair flowing wildly around a gorgeous face enhanced by skillfully applied makeup, the sight of Margo holding Sasha's baby daughter didn't quite fit. Which proved that appearances were deceiving. Margo was a natural with her little niece.

"Grab the coffeepot, Margo, and sit down. We must teach this innocent about seduction."

"Oh, what fun. I love bawdy chats in the middle of the day! And you are in luck, *ma petite*. I am an expert on the subject."

The look of glee that spread across Margo St-Pierre's features told Raquel she was in for quite an education indeed.

Chapter Seven

Cole's heart dropped to the pit of his stomach when he saw the precarious way she was perched on the six-foot stepladder, straddling the top rung.

"What are you doing?"

She jolted and the ladder wobbled. He grabbed the aluminum frame with one hand and her bare foot with the other. "You're going to break your neck."

"I was doing just fine until you scared the devil out of me!"

"I'll bill your father for exorcism rites. What are you doing?" There were no babies to photograph so he didn't see the need for daredevil balancing acts.

"I am taking practice shots, testing different angles. Now that you're here, why don't you lie across the cotton over there so I'll have a subject to judge by."

"*Lie* across the cotton?"

"Yes. You know, like the centerfold in the sexy magazines."

His eyes narrowed. "When did you ever see one of those magazines?"

She grinned. "I have wonderful girlfriends who have made it their mission to be bad influences on me."

"Remind me to leave that out of my report. I'd be

fired for negligence if your father found out you'd indulged in taboo reading material.''

"You are keeping a report on me?"

That stubborn, don't-mess-with-me look came over her face. She shoved her auburn hair behind her ears, and his grip tightened on the ladder.

"Either be still or come down from there. You're going to wiggle one too many times and fall off."

"I have perfect balance. I've done this many times before without a bird-dog security man interfering."

"Bird dog?" He was fairly certain he was offended by that label.

The flipped ends of her hair swished across her shoulders as she gave a jerky nod. Brown eyes shot darts of defiance...and challenge.

Man, she was incredible. He wanted to grab her off that ladder, to press her lithe body against his, to watch that stubborn irreverence change to smoldering passion.

What was he thinking?

"You did not answer me. Are you taking notes to send back to my father?"

"Not the kind you mean. But I have to have documentation of my time, the alarm system, the measures I've taken to insure your safety. Things like that."

"Oh. Well, that's all right then. Now, would you like to pose for me?"

The woman switched moods like a chameleon. "I think I'll pass."

"Party pooper. You could unbutton your shirt, mess up your hair a little bit..." Obviously getting carried away with the image, she gave him a very thorough once-over with those exotic eyes. His hand tightened around her ankle, and he told himself to head her off before they both ended up in very dangerous waters. Sexual waters.

His brain didn't summon the words quick enough.

"A pair of tight jeans, I think." Her gaze centered on that part of him which he knew damned well was swelling. "No, better yet, the slacks are a nice touch. Perhaps you could take your shirt all the way off and add a tie. The yellow one with the gray stripes would be a perfect offset with your skin tone, and—"

"Raquel?"

"Hmm?"

"No."

"No?" Amused disappointment colored her voice.

"No," he repeated firmly. For crying out loud, he was ready to combust.

"Pity. It would be a very good shot. You are a perfect subject for a calendar…wide shoulders and excellent muscle tone, no love handles around the middle, nice flat stomach, a—"

"Who are these friends of yours?" he interrupted tightly before she could finish cataloging his attributes. With the list heading on a southerly path, there was no telling what else she'd describe.

"Sasha and Margo."

That explained it—at least with respect to Margo. The woman was a bombshell with the kind of voluptuous curves that assured plenty of male attention—the type of woman who could tease and flirt and stir up a slew of trouble. And although he'd already figured out that Margo St-Pierre had a heart of gold, he wouldn't put it past her to do a little worldly tutoring.

"Maybe you shouldn't be spending so much time with those two."

Raquel laughed and swung her leg over the top of

the ladder. "Oh, but they have so much good information and suggestions to impart."

Cole swiftly anchored both hands on the aluminum frame when it teetered. Her sweet tush swayed enticingly as her bare feet found a sure toehold on each rung. Since he was forced to steady the ladder, her descent brought her right into the circle of his arms. When her foot found solid ground, she backed into him—deliberately, he suspected—pressing right into his pelvis, causing his erection to go from fairly impressive to rigid trophy size.

He leapt back as if scalded, narrowing his eyes as she coyly glanced over her shoulder.

"I could get used to a gallant man around the house."

He swore and turned his back. "Take a cold shower, woman."

Her laughter rang around the room. "Perhaps you should join me. You are looking a little hot."

Man, oh man, he'd sooner face the business end of a forty-five rather than this sexy heiress intent on flirting. Flirting, hell. The woman was waging an all out seduction war.

And damned near winning the battle.

RAQUEL WAS PEEVED at the inventiveness Cole used to avoid her. If she got too close, he took off in the opposite direction. Even now, he sat across the room, his concentration focused on the laptop computer.

She glanced at the closed door. The September heat had climbed and didn't show any sign of abating, even though the sun would be setting in a couple of hours. She thought of her precious petunias and fuchsias, sure that they were in dire need of a drink. One thing was for certain, the stuffy house could use a cross breeze.

And she could use a distraction from her overactive imagination and rampant hormones. Figuring out ways to initiate seduction was keeping her in a state of frustration…like a sneeze that wouldn't quite materialize, building, building, satisfaction and relief within reach, and then…whammo. Nothing. Only a teaser that made her want to scream.

Blowing out a frustrated sigh, she marched to the door, yanked it open…and froze like a thief caught dead to rights with the goods.

The newly installed alarm screamed like a banshee, placing her perfectly healthy heart in grave danger of failing. She didn't know whether to run, cover her ears or scream right along with the shrill din.

Neighbors streamed out of doorways to see what the commotion was about. Rattled, but at least over the worst of her paralysis, she shook her head and waved them back, then whirled around and shot Cole a disgusted look.

He walked over—taking his sweet time in her opinion—and punched in the reset code.

Her ears still rang from the cacophony of bells.

"I do not like my home rigged like this." It made her feel trapped, hemmed in, a feeling too reminiscent of her early years.

"Tough. I'm responsible for that sweet butt of yours. That means the alarm stays. You might as well learn to use it."

Raquel lost her entire train of thought somewhere around his "sweet butt" comment. When he pinned her with those steely blue eyes she was hard-pressed to remember her own name. The man might go overboard on security but he could make her heart flutter with only a look—and pull her erratic hormones right back to attention.

She took a calming breath. "It seems unnecessary for the bells to ring when going *out* the door. Shouldn't it be only if someone comes *in?*"

"Maybe I intend to keep better tabs on you."

She pressed her lips together as laughter threatened. "It still annoys you that I got out of Valldoria without your knowledge."

Cole put his hands on her shoulders and physically turned her toward the code pad. He hadn't been annoyed, he'd been damned impressed...and proud...and worried, if he were honest with himself. But he wasn't about to tell her this. No telling what she'd make of the admission. She had that impish expression dancing in her eyes that spelled trouble.

And he was not going to take the bait. It had required all his willpower to avoid her while still keeping his eyes on her. And she hadn't made it easy.

"This is the code," he said, surprised by the rasp of his voice. Patiently, he went through the instructions of arming and disarming the system—and got the distinct impression he was wasting his breath.

Her gaze was riveted on his hands.

"Are you paying attention?"

She nodded, glanced at him and swept her tongue over the seam of her lips.

He sucked in a breath. If that wasn't a deliberately provocative action, his name wasn't Cole Raul Martinez!

"Don't look at me that way."

"What way?"

"Like I'm the main course for dinner."

"Oh, dessert surely," she said, her voice sultry and full of invitation.

"What the heck has gotten into you?" The look in her deep mocha eyes was as timeless as blue skies over sunlit fields on a spring morning.

The look of a woman with sex on her mind.

His shirt clung to the damp line of his spine. He'd brought the wrong clothes, Cole decided. The sport jacket covering his weapon was way too hot. But around Raquel, he was always hot.

It suddenly seemed life-and-death important that he get out of this house, away from the temptation of the queen-size bed just down the hall.

And therein lay the bane to his very sanity. It was his job not to leave her unguarded. Although there hadn't been any recent indications that she was in danger, he couldn't afford to take chances.

Raquel ran her damp palms over her hips. Her mind was swimming with the various techniques Margo and Sasha had suggested. The lip-licking thing had certainly gotten a reaction, though not the one she'd intended. He appeared to be panicked rather than turned on. And he'd backed up a few paces—which wasn't the idea at all.

But Margo had told her that persistence was the key to any coveted goal. *Subtle* persistence.

"I see I have made you uncomfortable." She smoothed her hair behind her ear, took a step closer. "Perhaps we should have a small break and go out to dinner."

"Perhaps you should just keep your distance." His deep voice held a wary tone. "Better yet, don't talk to me."

She laughed. "Poor Cole. We have both had a busy

day and deserve to be waited on. Have dinner with me. I promise to be good."

"That's what I'm afraid of." Cole raked a hand through his hair. He had an idea she'd be damned good. And he wasn't talking decorum.

"I never would have considered you timid."

"Not timid. Smart." That sexy grin of hers was going to get them both in deep trouble.

"Chicken," she countered.

He fought the smile that tugged at his lips. "I should turn you over my knee for sass."

She laughed. "I am terrified. Let's go." She brushed by him, giving him little choice but to follow.

"Raquel?"

"What?"

"You forgot to set the alarm."

"You go ahead. I wouldn't want to spoil your fun."

"Woman, you're heading for trouble."

"I'm counting on it."

He closed his eyes and counted to twenty. It wasn't nearly far enough. Resigned, he unclasped his gun from his belt and dropped it into his boot. With more force than was strictly called for, he stabbed the alarm code and closed the door behind him, picking up his pace to catch up with Raquel.

She was wearing another one of those skimpy tops that exposed her midriff. Sleeveless and scoop-necked, it had a row of covered buttons down the back that begged a man to undo.

He dragged his gaze away from that temptation, only to be confronted with the back of her tight hip-hugger pants—and the tiny zipper that would only take a flick of the tab to have it lowering.

Man alive, he had to cut it out. Obsessing over undressing Raquel Santiago was taking bodyguarding way too far. He lectured himself that he was being paid to guard her *clothed* body.

And he knew his imagination was going to give him more sleepless nights. Especially since her fashion sense lent itself to more exposed skin than should be legally allowed.

They needed a solid set of rules of conduct. The problem was, it would end up being incredibly lengthy. Added to that, he was almost certain Raquel would take delight in breaking every rule.

He fell into step beside her, his eyes scanning their surroundings. Appreciative male gazes followed their progress, and they certainly weren't aimed at him. He moved closer, his jaw aching with the force of his clenched teeth.

Raquel glanced at him and slipped her arm through his. Her soft, plump breast pressed against his bicep.

He might as well give it up and fax in his resignation. He was precariously close to the edge and in grave danger of slipping over.

"You know, you would be much more approachable if you smiled instead of scowled at everyone this way," Raquel suggested pleasantly.

"The last thing I need is people approaching me."

"Oh, you are an unfriendly grouch. But I forgive you." She gave his arm a squeeze and waved as they passed the butcher shop. "*Bonsoir,* Tom. All is well with you, I hope?"

Tom preened and swept his hand over his bald head, a gesture that spoke of habit rather than insecurity. "Very well, Raquel, especially at the sight of such a beautiful *mademoiselle.*" He sketched a bow, his massive arms sweeping his knee like a knight of old.

"You appear to be friendly enough for the both of us," Cole griped. "So what's with you and Mr. Clean?"

"Mr. Clean?"

"The guy on the detergent bottle—bald head, tree-trunk-size arms."

"I am not familiar with that person."

"Obviously not your brand of cleaner."

"Are we going to have a debate about my house-keeping skills?"

"No."

"Then what is your point?"

"The guy on the bottle's a dead ringer for your Tom—who, by the way, appears to have a thing for you." He remembered the fiasco when he'd overreacted and aimed his gun at Margo St-Pierre. Of all the men who'd been present, Tom was the one most bothered by Cole and Raquel's living arrangements.

Raquel laughed. "Do not be ridiculous. Tom is madly in love with his wife, Eloise."

Cole didn't know what had gotten into him. He wasn't a man given to jealous tendencies. Then again, around Raquel, he was experiencing all sorts of firsts.

Especially those stray thoughts that had to do with babies, commitment and happily ever after.

"Where are we going anyway?"

"A small café about two blocks from here. They have a marvelous Italian menu, and the owner is a friend of mine."

"Male or female?"

"Does it matter?" Raquel glanced at him. His bouts of what could easily be construed as jealousy were cute so far because he'd kept it light. However...

"I must tell you, Cole, I am like a hummingbird set

free. Displays of control will set me off like an angry wasp."

"It's not my intention to control you."

She gave his arm another squeeze, feeling the solid press of his bicep against her breast. "Good. The friend is female. And you have met her. Mariana."

"Benjamin's mother?"

"Excellent memory," she praised. "Since Ben is but two weeks old, Mariana is not attempting to run the trattoria single-handed like she usually does. Luigi has forbade her to lift anything heavier then the weight of their son. She still runs the show, though. You will see."

The smell of garlic and herbs permeated the air from several doors away. Cole recognized Mariana right away. It wasn't hard. Short and plump, she held a baby in one arm and used the other to gesture dramatically. When she caught sight of them, her band-leading arm arced wide, inviting Raquel into an embrace.

"Raquel! Cole. Welcome. Have you come for a meal?"

"Yes. I have decided that Cole must experience the best Italian cooking the continent has to offer." She peeked inside the blanket and cooed over Benjamin. "Oh, he has grown like a weed."

Cole nearly rolled his eyes. It had only been a few days since they'd last seen Benjamin. He glanced over her shoulder at the baby. Still no eyebrows. Didn't look any bigger to him. Yet Mariana appeared to agree with Raquel.

"The ache in my arm tells me you are right." She snapped the fingers of her free hand, pointing. "Claude, *le vin* Bordeaux, *s'il vous plâit,* and bread sticks." Barely taking a breath, she turned back to Raquel and

Cole. "You must take advantage of the beauty of the evening and dine outdoors."

A tiny drill sergeant, Cole thought. Mariana definitely ran the show around here. She led them to a table for two draped in a red-checked tablecloth. Candlelight flickered against a glass pineapple-shaped holder. A delicate sprig of wildflowers rested in a fruit jar that doubled as a vase.

The ambience was cozy and inviting.

Cole held out Raquel's chair. She gave him a soft smile and thanked him with a gentle, fleeting caress of his arm, sending rockets of sensation right to his chest and spreading southward from there. He had an overwhelming urge to kiss her hand, but controlled it and sat down. The table was so small, their knees brushed. He spread his legs wide, avoiding contact. It was going to be a long dinner.

Claude showed up with the wine and fluted glasses, as well as the requested basket of bread.

"*Merci*," Mariana said, still hovering. "Luigi has prepared an excellent Chicken Piccata as the special. Or if you prefer, I will bring the menu."

"I trust Luigi. Cole?"

"Sounds good to me."

"Excellent," Mariana said. "I will leave you two to enjoy the sunset and the meal.... Oh, I almost forgot. Are we still having the poker game at your house?"

"Of course."

"I wondered, with a houseguest and all...." She glanced at Cole.

Raquel grinned. "Perhaps we can convince him to join us."

"Ah, a rooster among the hens. We must not tell Luigi, he will feel slighted...well, perhaps not. He has been dying to have Benjamin to himself. I do not think he realizes what he is in for.''

Cole heartily seconded that statement.

Mariana glanced up as another couple entered the patio. With barely a pause in breath, she snapped her fingers at Claude who immediately went to seat the newcomers. ''Back to work for me. Enjoy your meal. And I will bring the cigars for the poker game as planned so we may be decadent and daring.'' Like a whirlwind, Mariana bustled off to chat, orchestrate and show off her son.

''Cigars?'' Cole asked, brow raised.

Raquel shrugged and grinned. ''Margo's idea.''

''I thought you'd been cured of experimentation.''

''With cigarettes, yes. Margo assures us we do not inhale the cigar smoke into our lungs.'' She sent him a challenging look. ''Will that go into your report?''

Cole felt his lips pull into a reluctant smile. ''Not if I value my job security.'' Her enthusiasm and zest for new experiences was charming, although he doubted she'd get much enjoyment from the cigars. He had an idea that smooth olive skin would turn an unbecoming shade of green. But she'd have to find that out for herself.

He remembered the wistfulness in her voice when she'd talked about never having girlfriends while growing up. She was now making up for that lack, and he was happy for her.

He sipped the tart wine and took in their surroundings, etching it on his mind like a blueprint. A man stood in the doorway of the boutique across the street. Early thirties, Cole cataloged, five ten, dark hair, one hundred eighty pounds, casual clothes, expensive shoes.

''You are doing it again.''

"What?"

"Scowling at everyone who takes notice of us."

"Just being cautious."

"It is more than caution. You are a pessimist."

"My pessimism keeps people alive."

"Is that really a problem? Valldoria is not known for a high crime rate."

"That's because I see to it."

Her brow raised. His attention was focused solely on her, but she knew he was aware of every move and lift of a glass around them. She also knew that he wore a gun strapped to his belt, hidden by the lightweight sport jacket.

"What about now? You are here because of implied danger to my father."

"My batting average is good but not perfect. Nothing stays the same forever."

Raquel toyed with her wineglass, feeling a rush of worry over her father. Unfocused, her gaze drifted to the early evening sky.

The days were sunny and warm, but the nights held a slight chill. As the sun slipped past the horizon, she shivered, yet watched the splendor unfold. She wished she had the power to hold back the moon for just a while longer, to savor the moment when nature tinted the dusk sky her tenderest blue.

She was barely aware of Cole moving, until he draped his jacket around her shoulders.

Her gaze jerked to his waist. "Where is your gun?" she whispered. She wasn't certain of the European laws regarding concealed weapons. Besides that, the sight of an armed man would raise questions or, worse yet, create a stampede of distraught customers.

"In my boot."

Concerned over the safety of his foot, she asked, "Doesn't it slip around in there?"

His lips twitched. "The boots are special made. There's a pocket holster to keep it in place."

"Oh." Watching him assist her with the babies over the past few days made her forget who this man really was—highly trained and dangerous. A giddy thrill coursed through her body, speeding her pulse. "Are you ever without it?"

"No."

"Even in bed?" Whoops, there went the mouth overloading the brain again. His hand jerked on his wineglass, his eyes alert and suspicious…and wary.

"I thought you were going to behave."

"I merely asked if you wore the menacing thing to bed. I said nothing about joining you there."

"Raquel…"

"Okay, okay." She leaned back as Claude placed antipasto salads in front of them. Heavens, with the way Cole bristled every time she mentioned anything that could be construed as having the slightest off-color meaning, a person would think that he was the one with the inexperience.

Which was an absolutely ridiculous notion. With his dark hair, compelling blue eyes that promised both danger and delight, and broad shoulders that spoke of power and assurance, he would have no lack of willing women.

Herself included. Just looking at him gave her a giddy thrill. Pulling his jacket tighter around her shoulders, she lifted her fork and tested the antipasto salad.

She should at least wait until dessert to try Sasha's suggestion of the direct approach.

Although she had no experience in the matter, it seemed only right that a blatant proposition be delivered over something sweet, gooey and sinfully decadent.

Chapter Eight

Raquel leaned back in the patio chair as Claude removed their salad plates and delivered the main course. Thanking him with a smile, she picked up her fork.

"Have you heard from home?" she asked Cole.

"I call daily." He tasted the Chicken Piccata and nodded his approval.

"And?"

"Nothing new so far. Your father has stepped on somebody's toes. We're still checking on leads to the identity of the person or persons responsible for the written threat."

"That could take a while. He steps on a lot of toes." In business, Santiago was a no-nonsense shark. Abrupt with very little tact. Some would even call him a tyrant. At home, though, he was a different man. Gentle. Protective. Proud. Although he'd never once said "I love you," she knew he felt it.

And that made her worry increase, made her feel guilty that she didn't want to go home.

She glanced up, reaching for her wineglass, and her hand jerked.

"What is it?" Cole's head whipped around, scanning the patio for danger.

"Nothing." It shouldn't have amazed her that he would look for menace in every corner or gesture—and she was sure there was none. Still, her insides quivered slightly, a knee-jerk reaction like seeing an old beau after many years' separation.

But Cole was so in tune to her every move he would react even if she sneezed...probably certain a villain was at hand and should be held responsible.

She just wished he'd get a little more in tune to her sensual advances. "I thought I saw someone I knew."

"Who?" When she shook her head, he set down his fork. "Raquel, don't play games with me. I need to know who and what you see, everything you feel. No matter how insignificant."

"At least we're getting somewhere." She intended to tell him everything she felt. Or a certain version of it. And he'd given her the perfect opening. But it would have to wait a moment. "A man was standing at the end of the street. Or so I thought. When I looked back he was not there."

"Did you recognize him?"

"It was probably a trick of my imagination, but yes, I did. So you can relax. He looked like Lucian."

Cole's shoulders lost some of their rigidity. "Do you still see him on occasion?"

"No. Not since settling here."

With one last sweeping look that took in the boutiques, the cobbled street and the quaint patio, he picked up his fork. "What happened between the two of you?"

"He dropped me like a hot biscuit when I told him Papa had disinherited me."

"Jerk."

"No. He was sweet most of the time. And he played an important role in my life. He gave me the courage to leave home. For that I will always hold gratitude in my heart for him."

"Only gratitude?"

"Yes. He does not have the strength of character that I need in a man." Not like Cole, a man who could stand up against any odds, against her father even. "I must admit, though, I was taken aback by his reasoning. I have since wondered if he merely used the disinheritance as an excuse, if perhaps my father...or *you* got to him."

"Got to him how?"

"You know what I mean. I witnessed myself a payoff attempt between my father and Briana."

Cole shook his head. "None of us were that worried about Lucian. No money exchanged hands."

It rankled that they'd dismissed her choice of a potential lover so easily. Never mind that their unconcern had merit. "And threats?"

"My military does not make a practice of shooting kneecaps," he said dryly.

She shrugged. "Just a thought. It is almost easier to accept, rather than having to admit that I was only a trust fund to someone."

"Is Lucian any good at his art?"

Raquel didn't like to make light of anyone's aspirations because she knew how strong a dream could be. Still, she'd often wondered if Lucian had the drive and dedication to perfect his craft, to take it to its highest level.

"There is a certain spark to his abstract style of painting. He needs only to harness his energy, to trust his style and practice it. He is, how shall I say it...not as confident as he should be. He will change his style every other week, based on what he *thinks* people expect of him or what he thinks will sell best.''

"And you? If your photographs had not sold. What then?"

"I don't know. I have never considered that they would not sell. What I do pleases me greatly." Her shoulders lifted in casual unconcern. "I simply assumed it would please others also. Regardless, though, I could never stop photographing beauty and uniqueness. It is a part of my blood, I think, a chant within me that draws me to the camera from the moment I wake in the mornings."

"You are very talented."

"Thank you. I am fulfilled at least."

"And France? You like it here?"

"Yes. This is a beautiful village, and the people are wonderful."

"Valldoria is beautiful," he reminded her. "And the people aren't so bad if you give them a chance."

"Yes, but it is different." She pushed her plate away, leaned back in the chair and gazed pensively at the full moon riding low in the sky.

"I am treated differently because of who I am. Here, I am respected as a businesswoman. At home, if I had attempted to pursue this career, it would have only been viewed as a hobby. I would have been pulled in so many directions, expected to uphold obligations, preventing me from putting myself and my career first."

"That's hard to believe. Especially with your stubborn streak of determination."

"Determination suffers when constantly pounded by dissension. I love my family, but they make me feel like a puppet on a string. I have difficulty saying no to them, and because of that I am reduced to being their little girl...." She paused, running her fingers over the beaded moisture of her wineglass.

"Here I am a woman." Their gazes locked and she didn't look away. Deliberately, softly, her voice a sultry whisper on the night air, she added. "And I like being a woman."

Like a predator, alert and roused to attention by the scent of prey, Cole's spine went rigid. He didn't have any trouble reading between the lines of her quiet words. He was saved a response, though, as Claude hovered with a tray of desserts.

Although her head shifted toward the waiter, her gaze clung an instant longer. He watched, fascinated as Raquel considered each confection and settled on a white-chocolate cheesecake drizzled with rich caramel.

He shook his head when Claude turned to him.

Raquel arched a dark brow. "The desserts here are famous. Are you sure?" At his nod, she turned back to the waiter. "Bring an extra fork, Claude. I will temp him."

She didn't need cheesecake to tempt him. Her sexy lips, those exotic eyes and the flirty hint of bare midrif were temptation enough.

I like being a woman.

She toyed with her wineglass, her gaze fixed on him pinning him, making him sweat. Ruby liquid tippe against the glass as she lifted it to her lips.

Her slender throat worked on a slow swallow of po tent liquid. Deliberately, provocatively, her tongu swept the contour of her full lips, leaving them eroti cally slick, exquisitely tempting. The look in her eye went from casual to stunning in less time than it too to blink.

And that's how Cole felt. Stunned. To his very core

Around them, intimate conversations murmured, lovers touched, utensils scraped against ceramic. The moment spun out. Candlelight gently flickered against skin as smooth and supple as buttercream.

He couldn't take it. She made him nervous as hell, made him want. Want like he'd never wanted in his life.

"Don't look at me like that."

Her lips curved into a slow smile that held him spellbound, like a handful of starlight tenderly gathered and strung on a moonbeam. Enchanting. Glorious. Beyond words.

"We have already had the main course."

"And we've already had this conversation. You ordered cheesecake," he reminded her just as Claude placed the enticing wedge before her and stepped away. Couldn't the young man at least have the decency to linger? They sorely needed a distraction...or a chaperon.

"Perhaps I have room for both."

So much for the distraction. "Cut it out."

He should have known she'd do the opposite of what she was told. And it wasn't his imagination that she was deliberately practicing her wiles on him in a way that had nothing to do with innocence.

Her lips closed over a bite of cheesecake and despite his noble intentions, he found himself caught in her web of innate sensuality, found himself licking his own lips as if tasting the sweet caramel that clung there. She closed her eyes and moaned, as if on the gentle precipice of building desire, fulfillment just a stroke away.

Hell on fire! He looked away. *Get a grip, man!*

"This is incredibly decadent," she said. "Sure I can't talk you into a bite?"

"No." His tone was surly, sounding like a little boy who'd been told he couldn't have the prize.

Raquel laid down her fork. She felt giddy with feminine power. His blue eyes glittered with an inner fire that made her bold. She never realized she had this much nerve. And while she was riding on this high, she decided to push. She had no idea how long Cole would be staying.

And she could not let him leave without fulfilling her wish. He was a man she could trust, worldly, yet gentle, with a heart he kept wrapped against emotion. A man she'd admired, fantasized about, longed for…at a time when she was not free to pursue him. It was a bittersweet twist of fate that he was still beyond her reach—for different reasons now. Their time together could only be measured by a matter of days, or weeks, instead of a lifetime.

Still, she wanted to be the woman to break through his barriers, if only for a short time.

His scent clung to the jacket around her shoulders, shrouding her in his essence. Her fingers trembled and her heart pumped, but she ignored the signs of nervousness.

Her chest rose on an indrawn breath. "I would like you to teach me about lovemaking."

He shot straight out of the chair, knocking over his water glass. For an instant, the outdoor patio went silent as customers paused to locate the source of commotion.

The sounds of dining resumed. Cole summoned the waiter with a terse nod of his head, a command that had Claude nearly tripping over himself to arrive with a cleanup rag.

"Check please," he said tightly.

"Was everything...satisfactory?" Claude asked, concerned, appearing a bit rattled by Cole's brusqueness.

"Fine. We have an engagement."

Raquel raised a casual brow even though her heart pounded. "Well, that was fairly easy. I thought I was going to have to do more convincing."

He shot her a terse look. "Not *that* kind of engagement. Are you finished?" He took her elbow, ushering her to her feet, and without waiting for the check dropped several bills on the table, more than enough to cover their meals.

"Evidently I am." She waved at Mariana as she attempted to keep up with Cole's clipped pace.

They walked in silence for a few minutes. From the corner of her eye, Raquel noted the rigid set of his broad shoulders. She gave a mental shrug. She'd already jumped into the deep end—might as well swim the distance.

"I don't know why you are acting so prickly. I merely asked a question."

He shot her an incredulous look and kept walking, his suspicious gaze traversing the shadowy storefronts as if daring someone to make an untoward move. She nearly laughed. He looked like a man spoiling for a fight, like a man who'd welcome the violence.

"It is not good to keep emotions bottled up," she said casually. "It will send you to an early grave."

He stopped abruptly and swung her around to face him. Belatedly, she thought about her words. His father had gone to an early grave. "Cole, I am sorry. I didn't mean...I meant no disrespect to your father."

He frowned as if he had no idea what she was talking about, and proved it by saying, "What kind of game are you playing?"

She held his smoldering gaze, torn between flippancy and seriousness. And though she was utterly serious about her quest, she allowed a light note to color her voice. "I am merely attempting to solicit some advice. After all, you are an experienced man, are you not?"

He didn't answer. Just as well. She didn't want to know about his other women. "If you are uncomfortable with a hands-on technique of teaching, we can simply have the lesson orally."

He made a choking sound deep in his throat, stared for several heart-stopping moments at her mouth, then turned her back toward their pathway home and resumed walking.

In silence.

"Well?" she asked.

"Well what?"

"*Por Dios,* Cole, it is a simple enough question. You are acting like you are in pain."

"You have no idea how much pain," he mumbled. "This conversation is not only inappropriate, it's over."

"Who says we must be appropriate?" she persisted, even though the dangerous look in his eye sent a thrill through her that felt very close to fear. "There are only the two of us here. You may rest assured that what is said or done between us will remain private."

"In other words, you won't tell if I won't?"

"Exactly."

"Forget it."

This direct approach was harder than Margo and Sasha had led her to believe. Of course they hadn't counted on the depths of Cole's stubbornness. Or...

Perhaps it wasn't stubbornness. Humiliation rushed so quickly, so strongly, she felt light-headed. Her throat ached with frustration and something deeper. She felt the crook of his elbow tighten on her hand.

He stopped and drew her to face him. "Raquel?"

The man was entirely too perceptive. And her acting skills were incredibly rusty. She shook her head. "You were right. Let's forget it."

His palm caressed her cheek, so gently, so reverently, yet the expression in his fathomless eyes told her there was a world of reluctance in that touch. She closed her eyes, drawing on a lifetime of experience to mask her runaway emotions.

"Why me?" he asked softly.

"I thought we'd agreed to forget this conversation."

His thumb swept over her bottom lip. She had an idea he didn't even realize his actions.

"You are a beautiful woman, and I am flattered. But I'm not the man who should be your first lover."

"Who said you'd be my first?"

His raised brow both chastised and questioned. She shrugged, which was an answer in itself. He'd probably kept tabs on her anyway and would know she'd never taken a lover.

"Your first time should be with someone you love."

"So maybe I'm a little in love with you."

Cole felt his heart stop for half a breath, then start up again with a vengeance. She said the words flippantly. And she had that haughty heiress look about her, poised and cool, the one that no amount of probing could see past. The thought of being loved by this vibrant, exasperating, exotic-looking woman was a dream he didn't dare allow himself to think about too closely.

"Do not look so shocked, Cole. You must have known I had a girlhood crush on you. But you may rest easy. I was merely testing you to see if I could finagle getting my way. It is a curse of my regal training.''

She grinned and patted him on the cheek as if to say, no harm done. Or, just kidding.

It shouldn't have squeezed his heart this way. Music drifted out of the open doorway of a club. Latin music, he realized, a reminder of home. Perhaps that's just what he needed. A reminder of his duty, his position. Of who he was and where he belonged.

He inclined his head toward the sound. ''Want to stop in for a drink?''

''I thought you were in a hurry to get home.''

The closer they got to her house, to the proximity of her bed, the more he began to sweat.

''You work hard. We're out already, might as well enjoy the rest of the evening.'' And hopefully steer clear of the subject of sex and initiation...and the absurd longing that a woman like Raquel Santiago could actually be a little in love with him.

She smiled, making him feel ten feet tall. He'd only suggested they go for a quick drink, but the expression on her face was as if he'd offered her diamonds.

The minute they entered the club, he knew he'd made a tactical error. Raquel greeted every new experience with gusto, which kept his mind mired in images of the verve and enthusiasm she'd shower on a man in bed.

The *first* man in her bed.

He watched as she drank in the atmosphere, swayed to the rhythm of the music. The beat of drums and the pulse of organ and strings vibrated through him. Her animation was something to behold, so different from the reserved woman who'd grown up under the privileged, strict restraints of an heiress in Valldoria.

She greeted friends as they moved into the smoky, dim interior of the club, laughed and flirted and enjoyed.

She simply came alive.

And Cole couldn't tear his eyes away from her, even though he knew he should be searching the shadowy corners for strangers, or familiar faces even, for any hint of danger that might lay in wait for this woman. The woman who he was being paid to keep safe.

When the band struck up a new number, Raquel slipped her hand in his. "The salsa. I have not danced it in years. Come. We must not waste this amazing song."

He should not be on this dance floor, should not be staring at the erotic sway of her hips as she advanced and retreated, pursued, then beckoned him, their steps mirroring in a dance that had little to do with one-two-three, and very much to do with the rituals of age-old mating.

It was a sexy dance, a dance that teased and invited and filled his body with aching desire.

The sensual, challenging spark in her eyes drove him on. He hooked a hand low on her waist, drawing their hips flush with one another. She stared straight into his eyes. It was a wonder his feet could even keep the rhythm of the dance steps.

The music swelled and pumped through him. Her wildflower perfume, warmed by her body, filled his senses. Her skin glowed with a fine sheen of perspiration. His hand tightened at her waist, his fingers resting on the sensual swell of her hip.

Mesmerized, he dipped his head...and realized what he was doing. Jerking back, he saw the pain that flashed in her eyes, a flicker she masked so quickly, he might have imagined it.

She whirled away from him, still dancing within their allotted space on the floor, yet not with him at all. Male eyes focused on her; no man was immune to the sensual sway of this woman's body. The music stopped two beats before Raquel did.

Then, as if the uncomfortable moment had not passed between them, she smiled, stood on tiptoe and brushed her lips against his cheek.

"That was wonderful. Thank you."

Her chest heaved from the exertion of the dance, her breasts straining against that tiny excuse for a top. He tore his gaze away from the perky outline of her nipples.

He'd promised her the evening wouldn't end, yet he didn't know if he could survive another dance with her. As it was, he was hot and hard and ready to take her right here on the floor of a crowded nightclub.

"Do you want to get a drink?"

She shook her head. "We really should get home. The babies will be by early."

"Not up to a hangover, huh?"

"No thank you," she said heartily. "That is another experimentation that has cured me."

He looked at her, saw the slight widening of her eyes—the amusement—and knew exactly what she was thinking. Testosterone surged and his ego reared up in fighting form. He took her elbow and, as he ushered her to the door, spoke softly in her ear.

"Believe me, baby, if you and I *were* to experiment, I can guarantee you'd be far from cured."

The shock of his words shimmered between them like a taut, charged current. He saw her hands tremble as she laced her fingers together, saw the light of curiosity and determination that flashed in her deep mocha eyes.

She paused in the doorway, halting him with a delicate hand on his sleeve. "Answer me one thing. If you were not mired in some misguided notion of honor and nobility, would you *want* to make love with me?"

"Yes." The single, stark word was out before he could call it back.

Chapter Nine

Even before he fought his way through the profusion of vines and flowers hanging from the archway above the courtyard, Cole knew something was wrong.

His hand shot out, his forearm grazing Raquel's bare midriff. "Stay back."

"What is it?"

"The window's open."

"Of course it is. I opened it before we left."

"And I closed it."

She stared at him. "Are you sure?"

"Positive."

He reached for the gun in his boot, palmed it in steady hands, then carefully tried the front door. Locked. But that didn't mean anything.

He took the key from his pocket. "I'm going to check around back. Go next door to the bakery. Stay with Sasha until I come for you."

"Not a chance."

He spared her a glance, his features tight, dangerous, deadly. "This isn't a good time to argue with me, spitfire."

The idea that someone might have been in her home

rifling through her things frightened her. Sending Cole in there alone was even more frightening.

"No time is good for arguing with you. According to the rules, you are not to let me out of your sight. I am keeping you from breaking them. And we are wasting time."

She started to lead the way out the side courtyard gate. He grabbed her arm. "Do as you're told," he said tightly.

She faced him squarely. "I will, Cole. I will obey every order you give in the next few minutes. But I cannot hide next door, not knowing if you should need me, if I should call for help. I am the only backup you have available right now. I will not have you facing this alone."

A muscle moved near his jaw. "We're going to have a long talk about this stubborn streak of yours."

When he took her hand in his, the strength was protective rather than angry. They made their way along the narrow side passageway, the stones and mortar of the small house still emanating heat from a sun that had set hours ago. No fences separated Raquel's house from the bakery, which also doubled as living quarters for the St-Pierres. Lax building codes and limited space put the structures nearly within touching distance.

The backyard was almost as narrow; it enclosed little more than a flower garden bordered by a strip of gravel and a chipped birdbath that held several inches of stagnant water.

A clay pot lay broken on the back stoop, dirt scattered, the straggly fern she'd been babying resting in the rubble, its roots exposed.

Cole squeezed her hand—as though apologizing for the fate of the plant—then let go.

He checked the door, then inserted the key, turning the knob slowly. Raquel realized she was nearly plastered against his back and straightened to give him some room. The flashing light on the alarm box went from red to green as he punched in the code.

She felt as if she'd stumbled into the middle of a cops-and-robbers movie as she dogged Cole's steps from room to room. He held his weapon in both hands, pointing upward.

She bumped into an end table and froze at the grating screech of furniture against the wood floor.

Cole swung around, gun aimed.

Raquel's heart nearly jumped from her chest, breath lodged in her lungs.

He swore, lowered the gun and slapped a hand against the light switch. The muted glow from the hat-shaped lamp was warm and welcoming, banishing the surreal shadows of lurking danger. The house looked just like they'd left it.

Raquel let out the breath she'd been holding.

"The house is clear," he said, clipping the gun to his belt rather than dropping it back in his boot. "Check to see if anything's missing." He flipped open his laptop computer as Raquel rushed to her cameras, inspecting each one much like a mother hen might count her chicks.

Aside from the photographs, the cameras were her most prized possessions. They were all there, though. She relaxed, deciding Cole's suspicious mind had simply run away with him. He'd probably just forgotten to close the window, she thought, as she flipped through the pictures on the coffee table. Frowning, she went through them again, and then a third time to be sure.

"Cole?"

"What?"

"Did you do something with the photograph I took of you?"

"No. It's in the folder along with the ones of the triplets."

"No, it's not. It's gone."

He came over to her and looked through the folder himself. She arched a brow when he came up empty-handed.

"Habit," he dismissed.

"Why would someone take the picture of you?"

"I don't know. But I don't like it. It means somebody knows I'm here."

"Well of course people know you're here."

"Maybe the wrong people."

"Oh. But then, don't you think your absence has been noticed before now?"

"I've returned phone calls daily and planted interviews in the Valldoria paper in a manner that suggests I'm still there. My instructions are being carried out, and only your father and a few trusted men in my Guard know that I'm away."

"Could there be a leak among your military?"

"I'd like to think not."

She glanced at the window he'd shut before firing up his computer. "I suppose you'll be rigging those now."

"They're already tied into the system."

"Then…?"

"It malfunctioned," he said, his tone heavy with disgust and self-reproach. "And that's not acceptable, Raquel. I don't have the technology and equipment here that I need. I've had to make do with what I could get my hands on, and it's not good enough. A kid could breach this system."

"What now?"

"We need to return to Valldoria."

She looked down at her hands, picking at a snag in her nail.

Cole squatted before her, taking her hands in his. "It's my job to see that nothing happens to you. I can't do my job properly here."

"It was only a photo, Cole. And of *you*, not me."

"I have to report it," he said softly. "Whether we stay or go might not be up to me."

"I can't leave. I have obligations that are unfinished." He still crouched in front of her; they were at eye level. She met his gaze, imploring him with her own.

His palm cupped her cheek, gently swept the hair behind her ear. At last he nodded.

"I'll make some adjustments to the system, try something different. But I answer to the king and your father, Raquel. I can't go against a direct order if they insist on your return. All I can promise is that I'll do my best to stall them for as long as possible."

"Thank you."

"Don't thank me too soon. We're still unsure about the threats to Santiago. But if they follow through and make a solid move toward you, all bets are off. I'll be the first one to take you out of here, orders or not—over my shoulder if I have to."

Until now, like an ostrich, she'd made it a point not to dwell on the problems at home, hadn't wanted to know the details. It was odd moments like this that guilt swamped her, making her feel petty for wanting her life to stay the same. "Have I been threatened directly?"

"Indirectly. You've done a good job of keeping your whereabouts a secret."

"But if they discover me, will the babies be at risk?"

He nodded, his deep-blue eyes soft with apology.

Raquel felt a smothering tightness in her chest. "I will not risk any of them, Cole. Or my friends."

"I know." Cole rubbed his thumbs over her trembling palms. He saw the battle waging in her dark eyes. "I'll do everything in my power to make sure you can stay here." Which wasn't a whole lot. All he could do was sit and wait, like a duck in the reeds. Wait until the rebel made a move, or was uncovered and taken out.

So far, they had precious few clues to go on.

And it suddenly became very important that Raquel Santiago not be made to disrupt her newfound life. Important that she continue to cuddle and capture the babies of France in her unique, touching photographs, to ride her moped through the quaint cobbled streets, to do her own shopping, to enjoy the independence of having her own home, where she could let it get as cluttered and messy as she wanted.

Important that she not be molded back into somebody's idea of correctness, that she not be stopped from dragging any old thing out of the closet instead of having to spend days choosing just the right outfit befitting an heiress.

Important that she not be made to give up her freedom.

More than anything, he wanted to be the man to stand up for her rights, to see that her dreams didn't get lost under the expectations of a powerful family.

He hoped like hell he wasn't making a big mistake. A mistake that could cost lives.

Including Raquel's.

As Raquel had predicted, babies arrived early the next morning. Lilly and Cara, both in buckets decorated with pastel rainbows, were mugging for the camera. Cute as all get out, Cole decided.

"Oh, they are being so well behaved. Excellent! Wonderful! We must try them in the water," Raquel said without lifting her head from the viewfinder. "So far we've only gotten Hope in that pose."

"Want me to fill the pool?" He'd been roped into assisting again. In her breezy, sassy manner, Raquel had told him he might as well make himself useful as long as he was here. And because he was available, she'd been shooing the parents out the door, allowing them the rare treat of an hour to themselves. So far, they'd all gratefully taken her up on the offer.

He had to admit, he was becoming somewhat of a pro at diaper changes, pacifier hunts and bottle warming. He didn't like the costume changes, though. Manipulating those miniature arms and legs set his normally steady nerves on edge.

The ones who crawled gave him even more grief. Escape artists, he'd decided, damned near good enough to give Copperfield a run for his money.

"Almost there," Raquel cooed. "Let me just get this last angle and I will give you a hand with the pool."

A knock at the door blew the shot. Both babies swiveled their heads. When the caller didn't just walk in unannounced as most everyone else around here did, Raquel stepped from behind the tripod.

"Watch them, Cole?" She gestured to Lilly and Cara.

He stood. "No. *You* watch them. I'll get the door."

She patted him on the cheek. "My hero." Turning,

she spoke to the babies. "He is a very fierce bodyguard and we must not dent his ego."

"I heard that." Sassy woman was going to be the death of his good intentions. Especially the way she kept touching him every time he got within her reach.

He checked the small glass panel, hesitated, then pulled open the door, instantly recognizing the young man who stood on the front step. His gut tightened.

Lucian.

Cole took the guy's measure in a matter of seconds. Lean, pretty boy face, long hair past the shoulders flaunting convention, about five-nine, weak hands, high cheekbones and the rich skin tone of his Latin ancestors. Cole disliked him on principle.

This was the man who'd bruised Raquel's heart.

"Uh, is this the home of Raquel Santiago?"

Nice touch, creep. Pretend innocence in case there's nothing in it for you.

"Who wants to know?" His tone threatened, intimidated. The artist stepped back a pace.

"Cole," Raquel chided softly.

He left Lucian at the door, not caring if it appeared rude, and went to take over with the babies. As Raquel started to pass him, he stopped her with a hand on her arm.

"You don't have to talk to him."

"It is okay. I will only be a moment."

"And I'll be right beside you."

"The babies, Cole. Please."

She brushed by him, but he would not be dismissed. He lifted the buckets by their handles, babies and all. After the hair-raising day of kids getting loose from their baskets, he'd rigged the props with safety belts.

"Come on, soldiers," he said. "Duty calls and you've both been recruited. We have a body to guard."

Raquel turned when Cole eased up behind her. Her gaze darted to where she'd left Lilly and Cara. She relaxed when she saw that he'd placed them just to the left of the door—within reach, yet sheltered and out of harm's way. The stony, unfriendly look on his face told her he was prepared for a riot and spoiling for a fight.

She could have told him he had nothing to fear from Lucian. The minute she'd set eyes on the artist, she'd known there wasn't even a spark of feeling left.

"Lucian only wishes to talk, Cole."

He shrugged, staring straight at the younger man. "So talk."

"Alone," she stressed.

"Sorry. Privacy's not on the ticket for today."

Raquel didn't know whether to laugh or hit him. In the end, she decided to shake him up. She ran her palm lightly up his chest, licked her lips, gave him a sultry promise with her eyes alone, then turned back to Lucian, making sure her hips snuggled right into the cradle of Cole's pelvis.

She felt him jolt and decided it served him right for his dog-and-bone attitude.

"You must forgive him," she said to Lucian. "He is a possessive lover." Another jolt. Good.

"Oh," Lucian said, nervously clearing his throat. "I had hoped...I wondered if you would give me a second chance."

"Not on a bet, buddy," Cole growled.

Raquel rolled her eyes. He was getting into the spirit of possessiveness with a little too much zeal. "The question was directed at me, Cole." She felt him shrug against her back and nearly dropped her jaw when his hand slid around her waist, pulling her more snugly against the front of his body. His aroused body.

Her plan to shake him up had backfired. She was the one off balance.

She tested her voice, pleased that it worked. "I am still disinherited, Lucian." The slight tightening of Cole's fingers against her waist was the only outward show that he'd noticed her lie.

Lucian ducked his head. "It does not matter…in fact, I must apologize for the bad behavior I displayed six months ago. I worried that we would be nothing more than starving artists."

"I had more faith in my talents, Lucian." Her voice softened. "And in yours."

Lucian had the grace to look abashed. He gazed past her into the house. "I have seen your work on sale. You are doing well."

"Yes." The single word was born of pride, not boasting.

"Maybe I could watch you work sometime. For old times' sake. Your enthusiasm always gave me inspiration."

She felt Cole's fingers flex again and discreetly stepped on his foot, silently telling him to let her handle this.

"You cannot rely on others to keep you focused, Lucian. That determination must come from within."

He gave a sheepish grin. "You are not the first to tell me I am like a vampire, leeching the creative blood from others. I am very needy—and insecure." He shrugged. "Artistic temperament."

"Raquel?" Cole interrupted, intending to put an end to the tête-à-tête. It was becoming nauseating. "The kids are waiting."

"Yes. I really must go back to work, Lucian. I wish you luck."

"Of course. And…and thank you. Perhaps I will see you around?"

Cole had been about to slam the door in the guy's face. He checked the rude impulse. "Are you staying close by, Mr. Delgado?"

The artist seemed surprised that Cole knew his surname. Their paths had never formally crossed, so the chances of being recognized as head of the Royal Guard were slim. Using the last name would give the impression that he and Raquel were indeed close.

Intimately close.

"I have no permanent residence at the moment." Lucian glanced at Raquel, and Cole experienced a swift, barely controlled urge to take a poke at the guy. Lucian had obviously been angling for free rent as well as second chances. "I am staying with friends in Cannes."

"Ah, the home of the renowned film festival. Thinking of changing your artistic venue?"

Raquel stepped on his foot again, a silent chastisement, he decided. She'd told him about Lucian's wishy-washy attitude of chasing the current market. He shifted his fingers, caressed her stomach. The pressure on his foot eased.

Lucian seemed oblivious to Cole's snide tone. "There is a possibility of a commission at a filmmaker's home. It could launch my career overnight." Lucian dropped a few big names, tooting his own horn.

Cole wasn't impressed by the pitiful attempt. "Been in Valldoria lately?"

Obviously expecting more interest in the plum opportunity he'd just mentioned, Lucian frowned. "Some. Why?"

Cole smiled, more a baring of the teeth than nicety. Every time he took a breath, Raquel's hips rubbed against him. He was damned near about to explode. And this pantywaist artist who'd come sniffing around like he'd scented a dog in heat—or a meal ticket—wasn't improving his mood in the slightest.

"I am merely curious about men who come calling on my lady."

Lucian shook back his long hair, puffing out his chest like a preening peacock before an audience. "So, Raquel has mentioned me."

"Yeah. And like she said, she's not interested. Nice to meet you, buddy." This time he didn't harness the impulse. He closed the door in pretty boy's face.

Raquel stepped out of his hold and whirled around. "What in the world has gotten into you?"

He cocked a brow. "You started it, spitfire. You snuggle that sweet butt up to me that way, and I figure you're either asking for a public display of sex or you want me to play the game. Since I like my sex private, I decided to play the game." He saw her cheeks flush, saw her slender throat work on a nervous swallow.

"Hush. This is inappropriate talk in front of the babies."

"Now look who's complaining about improprieties." He tilted her chin up with a single finger, brought his lips within touching distance of hers. "The queen of nervy requests. I saw that take-me-baby look in your eyes when you announced I was your lover. And I'm not made of steel, lady, so be careful how you tease the animals. Sex is one area where I definitely don't play by the rules."

He turned away and strode across the room.

Raquel watched him, her insides a trembling mass of

hot, dizzying desire. It was a wonder she didn't melt right down into a scorching puddle onto the floor.

Cole Martinez had just given her a sizzling taste of the no-holds-barred side of his Latin heritage. In shocking, thrilling language.

Chills raced up and down her spine as her pulse throbbed, making her feel wild and reckless, and terribly unsure how to compartmentalize the runaway emotions. *Por Dios!* The look in that man's eyes! Exclusive. All encompassing. Mesmerizing. A look that both threatened and promised.

But he'd been warning her off. And although her goal to seduce this strong, tender, exciting, *reluctant* man scared her to death, she would not be deterred.

She wanted him with a fierceness that stunned, needed him more than she needed air to breathe.

And he'd just shown her another chink in his armor.

On a shaky, indrawn breath, she turned to retrieve the babies who were being uncommonly patient.

She wondered if Cole realized he'd just walked into her fantasy. Because she absolutely did *not* want him to play by the rules.

Chapter Ten

Cole's nerves were still on edge several hours later. He'd thought to scare the little innocent, erase that starry-eyed look that placed way too much responsibility on his shoulders.

The responsibility of being her first lover.

He should have known better than to second-guess Raquel. She was still going out of her way to brush up against him, silently inviting him to reach out and take what his heart and painfully aroused body desired. He knew without a doubt he was down for the last count. His storehouse of honor and reserve was all but depleted.

So it was a lucky thing that her girlfriends were streaming in the door, already placing side bets on who'd win the poker game. The women would create a much needed buffer.

Margo, buxom and statuesque, red hair flowing in wild abandon, led the way into the kitchen, with Sasha—short and blond and a little more reserved—trailing behind. The St-Pierre sisters-in-law were as different as night and day.

Mariana breezed in next—baby Benjamin absent—carrying the requested cigars. "I cannot stay long,"

Mariana said, helping Margo rearrange the kitchen chairs. "Benjamin will be wanting to nurse."

Despite himself, Cole's gaze slipped to her breasts.

Margo caught him at it. Her flame-red brow arched, but she didn't make an issue. "Eloise could not make the game. Perhaps you would like to sit in her place, Cole?"

"Oh, yes, do," the others chimed in.

Cole figured, what the hell. He didn't have anything better to do. He hooked a hand over the back of a chair and started to sit down.

"Perhaps we will spice up the evening and make this a game of strip poker."

He glared at the brash redhead. "Don't even start that."

Margo shrugged. "Just trying to help the romance along."

"There is no romance."

"Your eyes tell a different story, hotshot."

"You see what you want to see." But when Raquel came back in the room carrying ashtrays, Cole's gaze automatically shifted, as if drawn by a powerful magnet. His imagination went into overdrive as he pictured her tossing cards into the center of the table, then standing to slowly, erotically remove an article of clothing.

The sleeveless V-neck shell would go first, he thought. Four small buttons from cleavage to waist were all that held the sexy panels together. She would take her time, watching him, knowing exactly what she was doing...

Margo cleared her throat.

Cole jolted, and to his everlasting astonishment, felt his face flame.

Grinning, Margo aimed an imaginary gun at him, using her thumb and forefinger. "Bingo."

Raquel passed out the ashtrays, then trailed a hand over Cole's shoulders before she sat. "If we are truly going to smoke these things, we must open the windows, I think. Otherwise the babies who come tomorrow will be asphyxiated!"

Cole started to remind her that open windows would set off the alarm, but she gave him a discreet kick under the table.

He leaned over, spoke softly in her ear. "If they're such good friends, why won't you trust them with who you are?"

If eyes could shoot darts, he'd be an annihilated corkboard. He grinned.

"Okay you two," Margo chided. "This is a hen session. And although you are quite the rooster, Cole, you must act the part of a hen or be banned from the game."

He dragged his gaze from Raquel and arched a brow at Margo. "And just what do hens act like?"

"Oh, we will educate you. Men and sex will most likely dominate the conversation," she said with a sly twinkle in her emerald eyes. "Matchmaking possibilities have been known to come up also."

That's when Cole began to sweat. He'd had enough talk about education with regard to sex. Raquel gave him only small respites before blindsiding him with some new impropriety.

Now he knew for certain who'd been coaching her.

RAQUEL HELD her stomach and moaned.

"You're looking a little green there, spitfire."

"Shut up." She sprayed air freshener in the room. "Alarm or no, I am opening these windows! How can

Margo puff on those things? Oh, they are awful. I have rinsed three times with mouthwash.''

"It's an acquired taste."

"Yes, you went through yours easily enough."

He grinned and deactivated the alarm, shoving open the window. Raquel yanked open the front door and went to stand in the courtyard, drinking in the jasmine-scented air. Cole, too, had gone for a swig of mouthwash, but he didn't tell her that. She'd seemed almost awed that he'd smoked the cigar.

He stepped onto the courtyard and placed his hands at her shoulders, kneading the tension. She leaned against him.

"Mmm. That's nice."

"You're a decent poker player. Too bad I won most of the money."

"Do not brag, Cole. It is unbecoming. Besides, you would not have fared so well had I been in true form. With the stench of smoke, I should have asked for a handicap."

"That's golf."

"What is?"

"You've got your games mixed up. You give handicaps in golf, not poker."

"Oh, you are always so literal."

Raquel leaned against him, lulled by the gentle shoulder massage. The moon rode high in the sky, only a thin slice missing from its full face, giving it an oval appearance. A halo of yellow cast a shadow over it, making her think of the stories Antonio used to tell about the man who lived on the moon. He'd been teasing, of course, but she'd let her imagination run with the possibilities, built stories about the lonely man who lived there in the bright, glowing ball, stories that mirrored her own loneliness.

With the heat of Cole's body and the scent of jasmine surrounding her, she looked off into the distance, thought about that same moon shining down on her country, on her family's home. She wondered if they were safe, what they were doing. She missed them, but she didn't miss the restrictive life.

So why was she feeling so melancholy?

"What are you thinking?" Cole asked softly, his breath a warm caress on her neck.

"About my family."

"They're safe. I checked earlier."

She reached up and covered his hands. "Thank you. I feel so torn. Like I should be there to see for myself. Yet the other part of me knows there would be harsh words when they realized I was not home to stay."

"It'll work out. Perhaps enough time has passed that you will find acceptance rather than resistance."

"That would be wonderful. I would like to feel free to at least visit."

"Want to give it a trial run now? I can contact the pilot. The jet's still at Nice airport."

She shook her head.

"Sure? It'd make me a lot more comfortable security-wise."

"I have a deadline, Cole. The publisher is waiting for the photos. Maybe after it's done...."

Her words trailed off and Cole didn't push.

She leaned more fully against him, her shoulders resting against his chest, her hips snuggled against the front of his body. It felt as though she were made specially for his arms. A perfect fit.

He dropped his hands from her pliant neck muscles

and stepped back. He was getting entirely too comfortable. This woman had a habit of slipping right past his defenses.

And his defenses were pitifully weak.

"We should probably call it a night."

She glanced at him, her exotic eyes difficult to read in the shadows of the night. The slow smile, though, didn't bode well for his peace of mind.

"Is that an invitation?" she asked.

He closed his eyes. Honor was definitely overrated. "No. That was *not* an invitation."

She shrugged. "I'll take a rain check, then."

Looking up at the clear, star-studded sky, Cole prayed for rain—and knew that nothing short of the Great Flood would change the course they were heading on.

"COLE, WOULD YOU get this zipper for me?"

She presented him with her smooth, bare back, holding her hair aloft. This woman was a hell of a quick study. Just before she'd turned, those exotic brown eyes had held the light of challenge.

A challenge he didn't intend to accept.

Cole's hands flexed at his sides. This wasn't the first time she'd asked him to help her out with her clothes. He was starting to feel like a lady's maid.

A male, painfully aroused, lady's maid.

It would take every ounce of control he possessed to raise the teeth of the zipper when he wanted nothing more than to peel the figure-hugging, one-piece jumpsuit off her body.

His fingers brushed her hips as he gripped the metal tab. She made a soft sound deep in her throat.

Cole scowled at the zipper that went from waist to

neck. Gaped open, it didn't take a rocket scientist to know she was braless. No fancy lace straps banded her back. He had an idea the lack of undergarments was deliberate rather than an oversight. His palms began to sweat.

"Why do you wear stuff like this if you can't get it on by yourself?" he asked tightly.

"Oh, I could manage. It would just take longer, that is all. And I wear the jumpsuit because I love the way the material caresses my skin. So sensual."

"If you're trying to get a rise out of me, you've succeeded."

Her shoulders shook as she chuckled; his short tone obviously amused her. His gut clenched as the clingy material shifted. If he didn't hurry up, the damned thing was going to slip right down to her waist.

Grabbing the material at her waist for better leverage, he ripped the zipper upward as quickly as possible and whirled away. Then next time one of the babies spit up on her, he'd give her a damp rag.

And get an ice-cold one for himself. This hands-on fashion show was wearing him down.

It was midmorning and they'd already completed two photo sessions. The alarm had tripped both times as mothers—friends of Raquel's—had knocked for the sake of manners, and entered automatically, knowing they were both expected and welcome.

For the third time that day, bells screamed loud enough to bring the whole village to a halt. Sasha St-Pierre froze in the doorway and baby Carmen wailed right along with the din.

Raquel's demeanor went from the heat of sensuality to the blaze of irritation in less time than it took to blink.

She glared at him. "I am thoroughly fed up with this

disruption. I thought I told you the last time this happened to leave the damned thing off.''

He shrugged, unconcerned by her ire. "I figure if it goes off enough times, your callers will get up to speed on the rules."

"I will remind you once more. In my home, the rules are of *my* making. When we sleep, or leave, you may arm your annoying gadget. Otherwise, leave it off or I will rip it out."

"Raquel—"

"No, Cole. I am very serious on this. Those awful bells are upsetting the babies *and* me. This is not only my home, it is my place of business. And during business hours, the doors remain open!" In frustration, she stabbed at the code box. The bells still rang.

Cole grabbed her fumbling fingers and entered the code himself.

"I mean it. Don't you dare re-arm it," she warned.

He looked down at the woman who spit like an angry cat. She was something else—incredible, he thought. The desire to have her release all that passion on him— in bed—nearly overwhelmed him. He wanted to trace that sassy mouth with his tongue, map her incredible body with his lips and hands, draw the sweet, complex essence of her into his soul.

And the timing was incredibly bad.

He dragged his gaze away from temptation and looked at Sasha, who'd overcome her paralysis and had managed to soothe her baby daughter.

"Why have you installed an alarm, *ma chérie?*" Sasha directed the question at Raquel as she shifted Carmen on her hip. "You know our village is safe."

Still worked up, Raquel snatched up her camera. The light of combat in her eyes gave Cole pause.

"I didn't install it. Cole did. And he did it because I am an heiress whose fortune is greater than the Grimaldis of Monaco."

Those were the last words he'd expected her to utter.

For a moment there was dead silence in the small cottage. He saw her chin go up, saw the cool, empty facade slip into place. He knew her too well to be fooled. She was girding herself with armor, waiting for the inevitable awe to come over Sasha, waiting for the death of an easy, equal-footing friendship.

Waiting for the distance and reserve.

By the look on Sasha's face, she'd have a hell of a long wait. His hands shot out as Sasha thrust Carmen at him, leaving her own arms free to wrap around Raquel.

"Ah, *mon ami,* you are in danger, no? It is falling into place now…Cole's presence, his suspicions. The alarm. We must call a meeting, form a watch. The neighborhood will take turns to see that nothing happens to you."

"Nothing's going to happen, Sasha." There was wonder in Raquel's voice, a slight hesitation as if she dared not believe in the steadiness of her friend.

"Of course not. We will not allow it. You are our friend and we must stick together!"

Tears slipped down Raquel's cheeks.

"Ah, *chérie,* no." Sasha's voice wobbled. "You know I cannot allow anyone to cry alone."

Raquel laughed and wiped her cheeks. "I am being a ninny."

Sasha sniffed. "And you are in good company. If we cannot be ninnies with our friends, the world would be in very sad shape."

"Thank you," Raquel said softly.

"For what? Crying with you and having my nose become as red as Rudolph's?"

"No. For being my friend."

Cole felt a lump form in his throat. The scene before him was almost too touching to witness. He realized now, more than ever, that Raquel had made the right choice in coming to France. To take her away from here would be a crime.

To hold out any hope that she might go willingly would be a pipe dream.

His arms tightened around baby Carmen, who looked up at him with round, curious eyes.

"Well," he said to the baby, clearing the emotion out of his voice, "let's give Tia Raquel and your mommy some privacy."

RAQUEL'S GRUMBLING stomach brought her out of the darkroom. She'd forgotten about dinner. Again. Some hostess she'd turned out to be.

Her steps slowed halfway through the living room. Usually after a stint in the darkroom, creative juices were rushing on high and it took her mind and senses a while to adjust. Her work was both exhilarating and exhausting.

Tonight, however, awareness sharpened like the flick of a light switch. She looked around the room.

It was like coming home to serenity. A deep-red Bordeaux was poured and waiting in fluted glasses on the linen-draped dining table. An auburn glow from the hat-shaped antique lamp bathed the room in a warm glow as John Coltrane played softly from the stereo.

A late-summer storm had blown in while she was wrapped up with her picture developing. Thunder rumbled in the distance, rattling the windowpanes. Rain drummed gently against the tile roof, dripping from the eaves.

She felt the shift in atmosphere, the expectation, the tender storm brewing within her own body as her gaze sought out Cole's.

He stood by the table, an apron clutched in his hand, and pulled out a chair, silently inviting her to sit.

Everything within her softened. To have a man cater to her needs this way was the most exquisite kind of fantasy.

Now if she could only get him to cater to an entirely *different* need.

She moved across the room, reached out, feeling the need to touch him, to caress his face, to communicate the escalating emotions that tumbled through her with such magnitude she could hardly keep up.

He stepped out of her reach. "Sit. I thought you'd be hungry."

She smiled gently. "In other words, look but don't touch?"

She sat and tasted the salad. Cole joined her, but didn't offer a defense over his evasiveness. She didn't need the words, though.

His eyes gave him away.

He watched her like a man dying of thirst yet bound by invisible chains, bonds that kept the coveted glass of water just out of reach. She suspected a very thin, shaky line tempered that control, kept him from breaking free of the self-imposed restraints and seizing what he wanted.

Seizing her.

Trembling, scared…*empowered,* she could barely get the crisp lettuce past her throat. Her heart pounded and something tingling and wonderful raced through her veins.

Tonight would be the night. She knew it instinctively. Something this strong, this gripping, could not be one-sided. On the off chance that persuasion would tip the scales in her favor, she set her mind to doing just that.

"I must admit I am inexperienced in such matters…" Slowly, deliberately, she slid her fingers over the condensation on the wineglass. "But it appears as though you have set the scene for seduction."

His eyes—a blue as deep as midnight—held a quiet steadiness that made her tremble. The tempered heat in his direct gaze spoke of caution and confusion…and longing.

A longing that called to the deepest reaches of her being.

Raquel could easily put a name to the feelings that washed over her in rippling waves of excitement. The sweet blossoming of love.

"Don't read too much into a salad and glass of wine," he said, his tone deceptively cool.

It became increasingly important that she rattle that cool. Heat it up.

"It is more than salad and wine, Cole, and you know it." A haunting mix of saxophone and lyrics whispered from the stereo speakers, rising in tempo like wispy smoke from a building fire, filled with powerful images that expressed a world of dreams and desire.

"You are a civilized man, methodical, controlled, organized. Such a man does not take the care to use good linen, candlelight and music if the possibilities do not stretch beyond a quick meal. What is so bad about admitting that the great, cynical, suspicious Cole Martinez is a man who *can* be ruled by his passions?"

"You don't want to go there, spitfire," he warned in an unbearably quiet voice.

Buffeted by emotions that literally screamed for an outlet, she slapped a palm against the table. "Yes," she said boldly. "I *do* want to go there. With you." She hardly recognized the words that tumbled out, hardly recognized her own voice. "Why are you so afraid?"

"I'm not afraid. I'm protecting you."

"I am perfectly capable of protecting myself. Just look in my bedside table if you doubt me."

"Your..." His brows shot up, shifting his entire hairline. "I didn't mean *that* kind of protection."

Her eyes challenged him. "Are you shocked that I have a supply of condoms on hand? You shouldn't be. I told you I intend to do away with my virginity and I meant it. If not you, then it will be someone else."

His eyes narrowed. "Are you threatening me?"

"No. I am pushing, Cole, because you are too honorable and stubborn for your own good. And for mine. I may be a fool for leaving myself wide open like this, but I am willing to chance it. I ask for no promises. You warned that you do not play by the rules. I am calling you on that warning."

She saw the pulse beating at his temple, saw the veins stand out on his neck. Dear God, if he rejected her now, she would never live down the shame. But time was running out. There were no guarantees of how much longer they would be together. She could not allow him to leave without knowing the intimacy of his touch.

She wanted her initiation into lovemaking to be with the man she loved.

Emotion built, lodging in her throat. Wind-driven rain pelted the windowpanes. The clock on the mantel ticked, keeping time with the incessant throb that trembled through her body. She felt weepy and hated the weakness, hated the strength of the wanting. She'd spent a lifetime of dreaming, of feeling as if she was on the outside looking in.

At last she'd learned to take life into her own hands, to make the dreams happen. Without apology. Without hesitation.

This, the last of her emergence as an independent woman, a woman in love, was the most difficult hurdle she'd tackled.

And the most important.

"Please, Cole. I ache, and I..."

Before she could even finish the words, his chair skidded across the floor. He came around the table and hauled her to her feet, his hands gentle where they wrapped around her arms, his expression just the opposite.

His sigh was strained, barely controlled. "Be sure. Damn it, be *very* sure. Because if we start this, I won't stop." Softly now, his voice a mere rasp in his throat. "I won't be *able* to stop."

"Then don't. Teach me, Cole. Show me...."

Chapter Eleven

Her voice trapped in yearning, she held his gaze. The music swelled, and the power of the melody called to her.

As did this man.

She had no misgivings over what they were about to do.

She went into his arms, eased up against his body. A body that radiated strength, virility and a gentleness that nearly melted her soul.

His head lowered, the sure pressure of his lips like a balm to the ache that hovered on the wings of anticipation. So warm. So right. She opened her mouth, wanting more. The sweep of his tongue was subtle, not a storming of her defenses, but a careful, thorough foray that left her shivering.

She felt him shift, felt the press of his knee between her legs, and instinctively began to move, pushing against his thigh in an effort to assuage the throbbing that was both pleasure and pain.

Cole felt as though he were on fire. The pressure was almost more than could take—the responsibility. He would be her first. She was offering him a gift he didn't deserve, a gift he could no longer refuse.

And he was determined to make it right. To meet every one of her expectations and take them one step beyond.

And that meant taking it slow.

He broke the kiss, resting his brow against hers, eyes closed, a hundred different feelings fighting for control inside him. "One last chance," he murmured.

"It is what I want, Cole. Make love to me."

He groaned. "That did it. I'm a goner."

He bent and swept her in his arms, striding toward the bedroom. If he didn't get a bed beneath them soon, the strength she'd accused him of having would likely disappear sending them both into a heap on the floor.

This woman made him weak. And she made him want. Want like he'd never wanted in his life.

Her confidence and nerve impressed him, her sensuality nearly brought him to his knees. He'd beg—but that wasn't necessary. She'd offered.

And even knowing it was wrong, it seemed life-and-death important that he accept that offer.

She clung to his neck, kissing him wherever she could reach, making the navigation of her bedroom an iffy thing. He waded through the discarded clothes decorating the floor and eased her to her feet at the side of the bed.

Her wildflower scent permeated the room, alluring and sexy, teasing his senses and firing his imagination with every breath he took. A spill of powder and an open bottle of perfume on the dresser added strength to the fragrant air.

"Are you always this slow?" she asked, breath trembling, hands unsteady as she reached for the buttons on his shirt.

He caught her wrists gently and shook his head. "Slow's the best way."

"I don't know if I'll last. I am unused to these feelings. They are...I cannot describe it. Like butterflies stampeding."

He felt his mouth quirk. "Butterflies *stampeding?*"

She licked her lips. "Flying at warp speed at least."

The quirk turned into a gentle smile. "We'll settle them...in time. And then we'll stir them up again. Turn for me."

"What?"

"Indulge me. I've spent all afternoon imagining taking that zipper down."

She presented him with her back, looking over her shoulder, holding his gaze. He doubted she had any idea what that pose—that look—did to him. She was both an innocent and a siren.

Slowly, he brushed aside the hair at her nape, pressed his lips there.

Raquel shivered. Like a vibrant rainbow shimmering against the pall of a gray sky, that tender kiss on the back of her neck surprised her, filled her with glorious wonder.

She felt cool air caress her skin as the zipper parted, felt his knuckles skim her spine like a whisper-soft breeze.

Her heart soared and her knees bumped up against the side of the mattress, seeking something solid and stabilizing lest she melt like liquid silver into a puddle on the floor.

"You're shaking," he said softly, his breath warm against her neck, raising goose bumps on her skin.

"Yes," she whispered.

His hands stilled, then he gently turned her to face him, searching her features. "Are you afraid?"

"Yes. But it is a wonderful fear. An excitement. Yet..."

"Yet what?" His fingers combed through her hair, toyed with the delicate shell of her ear.

"I feel foolish, as if I might disappoint you."

"You could never disappoint me. The biggest danger here is that I won't make it good for you. You deserve so much. So much more than I can give."

She shook her head. "I am not asking you for promises, Cole. I trust you. I want it to be with you. Need it."

She saw his eyes flame at her words. His gaze never left her face. Even when he touched his lips to hers, they remained open, watching, gauging, enjoying, inflaming. With his thumbs, he eased the clingy material of her jumpsuit over her shoulders, down her arms.

And still he watched her, mouth clinging, hands teasing.

The power of that single-minded gaze transfixed her, the impression burning into her memory, sealed there forever. She knew without a doubt she'd call that look up many many times in the years to come.

And it would have to be enough.

Pain, swift and stinging, swept through her, because she knew that what they would share here this night would not last. He would leave, and she would have to let him go.

"Easy," Cole murmured against her lips. "Relax. Just feel." He felt her desire and her surrender, but he also felt her desperation.

And knew its cause. For an instant reality had intruded on their paradise. And as much as he'd resisted, fought to stay out of her arms, if he had to leave them now, he thought he'd die.

With the jumpsuit pooled around her waist, his palms gently tested the weight of her bare breasts, his thumbs sweeping across her taut nipples. Her breath hitched on a sob, firing his ego and making him feel like the greatest guy around, able to evoke such emotion.

"Stage two," he murmured. "Let's get you out of these clothes." Slowly, like uncovering a brightly wrapped, much coveted package one inch at a time, he lowered her stretchy jumpsuit to her ankles. She braced a hand on his shoulder as she stepped out of it.

He nearly lost his control when he got a look at her panties—if they could be called such. They were a mere triangle of lace held in place by minuscule ribbons of elastic.

Firecracker red. A red so hot it practically sizzled.

And Cole was burning up.

"Man alive, spitfire. Those ought to be illegal."

"They ought to be gone," she said, desperately sucking air into her lungs. The skill of this man's lips and hands was almost too much. She'd never imagined a woman could feel this way, never imagined a man could push her to the edge so thoroughly, so expertly.

Slow was well and good, but she'd had enough. She whipped the panties off herself, thinking to hurry him along, and reached for the buttons on his shirt.

He stepped back a pace. "You're hell on a man's control, baby." His eyes roved her naked form, appreciating, worshiping.

Raquel nearly screamed in frustration. "*Por Dios,* Cole! I am on fire."

"But you can get hotter." When his lips took hers once more, there was a world of patience in the touch.

He eased her back against the mattress, laid her amid the rumpled sheets that smelled of her unique sexy scent.

His fingers skimmed her breasts, her arms, lightly trailed over the backs of her hands. He straightened and reached for the lamp, twisting the three-way switch with one hand while the other dealt with the buttons of his shirt.

"Cole...?"

"We need the lights low. Not off, because I don't want to miss an inch of your sweet body." With his gaze alone he caressed her. Dropping his shirt to the floor, he unhooked his belt. "We're going to make the world go slow tonight." His voice rasped deep in his throat. "Real slow." He kicked away his pants.

Raquel drank in the sight of his virile body. His shoulders were broad enough to carry the weight of the world. A sprinkle of dark hair dusted his chest, and tapered downward.

He stood before her, fully aroused, allowing her to look, to become familiar with his body, to banish her fears.

And Raquel thought he was the most beautiful sight she'd ever beheld. The shadowy light from the bedside lamp created an ambience of sensuality, a reminder that the bedroom was a place were lives were shared, where dreams and hopes were built.

And if those dreams and hopes were not realistic or possible, it didn't matter. The real world was far away. For a while it could not touch them.

Rain drummed on the roof as the storm built in intensity. And not only on the outside.

He bent, opened the nightstand drawer and located

the condoms she'd told him would be there. His brow arched at the number of them.

"Expecting some long nights?"

"I like being prepared."

She held out her arms, and he eased into them, sweeping her on a journey of discovery, a journey of touch and taste and scent.

He taught her about a pleasure so intense it was almost pain. She gasped, writhed against the sheets, urged him to quench the raging fire that stunned and confused and promised. In her madness, she might even have begged.

And still he took his time, leaving no inch of her untasted, untouched. When he kissed her in the most intimate way imaginable, Raquel nearly came up off the bed.

She cried out, sensations rushing so fast, so hard she thought she'd faint. She couldn't take it. She was coming apart, not by slow degrees, but in one single, glorious explosion of overly-sensitized nerves.

The unbearable pleasure shattered into a burst of color, a crimson, molten intensity that left her wrecked and weepy and still aching for something…something elusive, something she didn't understand, could not put a name to.

She heard herself cry out Cole's name, marveled that the voice even belonged to her. Her nails bit into his shoulders, gripping, tugging.

He seemed to understand her plea, her confusion. His torso was damp, sliding against her as though they'd both been bathed in oil, the hair on his chest teasing her nipples as he eased up her body, covered her.

"Hold on, spitfire. This is the rough part."

She didn't understand his words, didn't care. Her hips arched, seeking, wanting, demanding.

She heard the crinkle of foil, caught a flash of red as he discarded the square package. She felt him press against her, felt the stretching, the fullness, felt impatient and out of control, wild and wanton and beyond reason. She arched into him, and sucked in a breath at the slight sting.

Cole swore and cupped her bottom, holding her still. "Easy. Give it a minute."

But a minute was too long. Because the sensations were building again. Stronger than before. It wasn't possible, but there it was.

Her breath heaved, her fingers fisted in his hair as she sought his lips. "Go. Hurry," she panted against his mouth. "Show me everything."

And he did. Slowly at first, and then with building intensity. Her eyes fluttered closed, as their bodies strained.

Cole felt the pulse of her femininity, felt those erotic muscles clutch him, squeeze him. Sweat beaded his lip as he fought to hold off, fought to prolong the pleasure that was almost too much to bear. Her wild response, her total surrender, made him feel like a powerful warrior, filled him with an intensity he'd never experienced before.

She made him strong. And she made him incredibly weak. He wanted to fill her up, give her all he had to give. Forever. But need outpaced his intent to prolong, driving him faster.

He felt her shatter beneath him, felt his own release roar through him with the force of a tidal wave slamming against a wind-swept shore.

The instant her name ripped from his throat on a

hoarse shout, he knew the armor he'd used to shield his emotions had cracked.

And that scared the hell out of him.

COLE SHIFTED to his side and drew her against him, pulling the sheet over them.

He felt, rather than heard her chuckle.

"What?" Laughter on the heels of earth shattering lovemaking could easily damage a man's ego.

"The spread is on the floor. It looks as though a war was waged in here."

Her hand stroked his chest and he felt his body react to that light, exploring touch. He covered her fingertips with his own. "A war, hmm? Did we win?"

"I certainly did. Thank you, Cole," she said softly.

He closed his eyes, unable to describe how those words touched him, how they devastated him. He had a black belt in karate and had been trained to anticipate the unexpected, the unknown.

He hadn't anticipated what making love with Raquel would do to him. His heart felt heavy, yet his words were light. "We aim to please."

She snuggled against him, kissed his jaw. "And what a magnificent job you have done. Why has no woman ever snapped you up?"

He stared at the ceiling, trying to ignore what the press of her naked body was doing to him. "Do we really want to get into this now?"

"Well, no, I do not want particulars of your other women. I only want to know you."

"I'd say you know me pretty well."

"I am not talking about sex." She placed her hand over his heart. "I am talking about right here."

He didn't dare examine that vital organ too closely.

Because if he opened up, let the emotions out, he might not survive, might not be able to keep them in perspective.

The wanting for what he could not have would be too much to handle. He'd compromised his job and his integrity by making love to her, a woman who was his responsibility. A woman who was out of his reach.

She was a free, independent woman, yet a perverse nagging in his soul reminded him that he had nothing to offer her. No riches. No royal title.

He owed her the truth, even though it would widen the chasm they'd both ignored by taking this step in the relationship.

"I have a full life, Raquel. A job I love, with prestige and power that I feed on. Even when I was in the States, I always knew I was working toward the day I would step into my father's shoes as head of the Valldoria Royal Guard. It was my lifelong dream."

Her hand curled over his heart. "Fulfilled dreams are wonderful," she said softly. "Even though they can create a world of loneliness. Our country is very lucky to have a man so dedicated to protect her."

His hand fisted against the sheet. Yes, fulfillment could bring loneliness. Especially when a man allowed himself a taste of the forbidden. A taste he'd likely never forget.

"When things are settled, when there is no longer a threat to my father, will you come back?"

"Raquel…"

She put her arms around him, holding him as if she feared he'd vanish. "The company jets are at your disposal. Surely you can take time off. Weekends, perhaps?"

"Is that what you want? Stolen moments? An affair?"

No, Raquel wanted to scream, yet she kept her silence. She'd promised him there'd be no strings. She'd miscalculated, though. She hadn't considered the strength of her regrets.

"It is a good compromise."

"What about my integrity in your father's eyes? He'd find out that I was flying off to spend the weekend in bed with his daughter. I can tell you right now that's not your family's idea of acceptable treatment for a first-class heiress. How long do you think my job would last?"

Oh, the impossibility was so painful. She could not ask him to risk his position, nor could she expect him to give up his dream. Even though everything within her begged for her to ask.

But she wouldn't.

Just as he wouldn't put her in the same position, the position of having to choose.

She placed a gentle kiss on his chest. "I asked for no promises, yet I find I am about to renege." She felt him stiffen and forced a light note to her voice. "I feel my education is still a bit lacking. Since our time is limited, I am after exacting your vow to remedy that."

His brow rose. "Have I just been insulted?"

"Oh, no. I only meant that you were the one who did all the touching." Her hand slipped from beneath his, moving downward.

He stopped her. "A man needs a little time to recuperate, spitfire."

"By the looks of you, I think you are fibbing."

She saw him grit his teeth as her hand evaded his

hold, continuing on in exploration. "I'm trying to be a gentleman, here."

"I never asked for a gentleman. I distinctly remember asking for the man who did not play by the rules."

"Rules have nothing to do with the fact that you're probably sore."

"I am not sore." She felt swollen and a bit tender, but the smooth press of nakedness, skin to skin, was causing the heated rush to begin anew. "The fire is building again...."

"Raquel—"

"I want to touch you, Cole. To kiss you in the intimate way you kissed me." She glanced at him, feeling both bold and shy at the same time. "Is that...I mean, could I?"

"Hell yes, but..." His words were lost on a sharp, indrawn breath as her fingers brushed him, tentatively at first, then with an expertise that took him right to the edge with a swiftness that stunned.

She raised up on her elbow, her breast grazing his side, his belly, her breath hot against that part of him that ached. His fingers tangled in her hair, clutched, as her lips closed over him.

She made love to him in a way no other woman had. With complete trust, her sole attention on his needs.

He wanted to stop her. He'd never allowed anyone to have such control over him, never allowed anyone to get so close. The job had always come first and he wouldn't chance losing his edge to soft emotions.

Yet Raquel sneaked right past his good intentions, his strict vows. The tickle of her hair against his thighs, the clever, torturous, innocent talent of her tongue, wiped his mind clean of everything but the exquisite pleasure that nearly paralyzed.

He couldn't take it. Could not get enough.

"For the love of—" His voice, like grating sandpaper against an inflamed throat, eluded him. He reached for her, forgot to temper his strength and jerked her beneath him.

This time there was a desperation to their lovemaking, an underlying tension to cram a lifetime into what little time they had left.

Raquel fed on that sweet edge of madness, setting aside all thoughts of an empty future.

A future without Cole.

He crushed his mouth to hers again and again, his hands racing over her, leaving a trail of fire. Fingers tangled as they both struggled with the condom.

Hurry, her mind screamed. *More.* Her hands both impeded and helped as they each frantically struggled with the protection.

Lips clinging, breath heaving, she met his aggression, matched it, her mouth devouring every part of him she could reach.

And still it wasn't enough, wasn't fast enough. She wanted to be possessed, to possess in return.

In a move both agile and electric, she rolled with him, breath ragged, and rose above him. She heard him swear, felt his hands flex around her hips as she sheathed him inside her in one fluid stroke.

For a split instant she stilled, feeling magnificent in her power. He filled her completely. Not just physically. Even in her spiraling pleasure she understood this.

She bent down to press her mouth to his, knowing that this man alone had found the way to her heart.

And when the physical was no longer there, he would remain.

Forever in her heart.

WHEN THE PHONE rang at five o'clock the next morning, Raquel sat straight up in bed.

Alert as only a man with his training could be at this hour, Cole swung his legs over the side of the mattress and snatched up the phone.

Listening to the one-sided conversation, Raquel felt a sense of foreboding.

Something was terribly wrong.

His words were terse, his voice commanding, questioning, his spine rigid. She got up and reached for her robe, hovering next to him, her heart pounding.

"What is it?" she asked the minute he replaced the receiver.

He stood and jerked on his pants. "A letter bomb. Delivered to the estate."

"*Madre de Dios!* My father. Is he hurt?"

He shook his head, his jaw tight.

Panic whipped through her. What was he keeping from her? "Talk to me, Cole! If not my father, was anyone injured?"

His distraction cleared and his eyes softened. Gently, he cupped her cheek. "I'm sorry. I shouldn't have frightened you that way. I should have chosen my words more carefully. Your family is unharmed and well guarded. My men were on the lookout for suspicious packages, unfamiliar people. The missive was intercepted and defused immediately."

Raquel released a breath and leaned into him. She saw his preoccupation, felt his gentleness to shield her war with his need for action.

And suddenly, Raquel regretted her stubbornness that had kept Cole from being in Valldoria, regretted that she herself wasn't there to touch her family members, to see with her own eyes that all was well. Although they had their differences, the strain was not born of meanness. A disagreement over life-style did not cancel out love.

What if the security personnel had been less watchful? What if the bomb had actually made its way into her father's hands? And thinking the worst, what if she'd lost her father without having had the chance to say goodbye? To say "I love you"?

The thought was intolerable.

"You okay?" Cole asked softly.

Raquel tucked away her roiling emotions and nodded. She knew Cole needed to leave, that even more than needing to, he *wanted* to. This was his job. A job he was good at. He had people depending on him.

And just as Carlos Santiago had wanted the best to come and get her, Raquel, too, wanted the best man available seeing to her father's safety.

And Cole was the best.

But because of her, he was torn.

She placed a hand on his bare chest. "You must go."

"I can't leave you unguarded."

"I know. I will come with you."

He stared at her for a long moment. "What about your photos? The last of the layout?"

She forced a smile. "You will simply have to prove how good you are at your business and clear up this unrest quickly."

"I'll know more when I get there...but I can't guarantee how long it'll drag on."

"I trust you," she said softly, calculating the time frame. Her deadline was looming, but she was a little ahead of schedule. A week wouldn't ruin her goal. And she needed this opportunity to reunite with her family.

She also needed the time to resolve herself to freeing Cole.

"I will reschedule the babies. Will a week be sufficient?"

"I don't know."

She searched his eyes. "It is all I can promise, Cole."

Like a bright-red circle on the calendar, she would count the days. But for her own peace of mind, she had to give a firm date. A date for the heartbreak to begin. A date when she would once again have to learn to survive. On her own.

Cole nodded. "A week," he agreed, wishing he could just wrap her in his arms and run with her, someplace safe, someplace private where there was only the two of them. But that wasn't possible.

He had the right to shield her from bodily harm, but that's as far as his rights went. He couldn't shield her emotions. And her emotions were shining like a beacon from her velvety-brown eyes.

He knew she was concerned over her family, yet at the same time already dreading the imposed restrictions they would unknowingly place on her. Not out of maliciousness, but because of who she was, who she'd been.

Expectations she would wilt beneath.

Seeing her so alive and vibrant here in France, he couldn't bear to watch that light fade away to darkness, couldn't bear the thought of her feeling imprisoned in a land that he called home.

If he didn't have a suspect in custody by the end of the week, he'd send a trusted man back to France with Raquel.

Knowing that the man wouldn't be him was like a white-hot knife twisting in his gut. By this time next week, he would have to tell her goodbye.

He couldn't give up his life in Valldoria.

And he couldn't ask her to share hers with him there.

Royalty did not live happily-ever-after with a body-guard, no matter how much prestige that bodyguard had.

"I'll call and schedule the jet," he said. "Can you be ready within the hour?"

"Yes. When you are through on the telephone, I will need to use it to rearrange my schedule."

"It's five o'clock, spitfire."

"I know. Margo is up before the rooster. I will dispatch her to do the calling. We can even persuade her to take us to the airport if you like."

"Sounds good. It'll save time if the pilot doesn't have to come get us."

She nodded. "I will arrange it. Now go make your telephone calls and play with your spy gadgets on that laptop. I have packing to do."

"Okay." Cole hesitated, placing a soft kiss on her brow, then swept up his discarded clothes and went to the kitchen to use the phone.

He didn't know what made him deactivate the alarm and open the front door.

There, tacked to the wood, was the missing photo that had been taken from Raquel's files.

The photo of him.

Scrawled across the face was a single word. *Boom.*

His first, unprofessional instinct was to rip the crude warning from its anchor and crush the thing before Raquel or one of her neighbors wandered out and saw it. Thankfully, he checked the impulse at the last minute.

He'd screwed up enough as it was.

Reining in his emotions, he followed procedure and donned a pair of gloves, then retrieved a plastic bag and carefully placed the tack and the photo in the protective covering, his mind turning over every possible meaning.

By using his photo, it appeared that the warning was

aimed at him. A polite criminal, for crying out loud? Giving him a fair chance to play the game?

Damn it, it wasn't like him to allow anyone to get the jump on him like this, and Cole knew the bile-raising bite of fear.

At the same time a letter bomb had shown up in Valldoria, a defaced picture was being delivered in France.

Right to Raquel's doorstep.

Cole had enough wits left to know the scheduling wasn't coincidental.

Now, the sixty-four-thousand-dollar question was, had the plan been orchestrated by a single perp? Or could there be a militant group of God-only-knew how many? Glaringly obvious, though, was the message.

They were merely toying with him, laughing at how ineptly he'd handled the investigation so far, how easily they'd breached the premises, both here and in Valldoria.

Even more chilling, whoever was behind the threats to the Santiago family knew exactly where Raquel was.

Next time, it wouldn't be an inanimate object.

Next time, a life would be lost. And that life could easily be Raquel's.

His fingers tightened around the plastic as he shored up the walls around his runaway emotions.

There would be no more mistakes.

He scanned the quiet cobbled streets. In the fragile stillness of dawn, his voice was deep and low and dangerous.

"Okay, buddy," he said to his unseen opponent. "Let's play."

Chapter Twelve

Margo stood beside her sporty Alfa Romeo, the trunk open. "It will be a tight fit," she said, "but it is not far to the Nice airport."

"I travel light." Cole placed his duffel in the small compartment. "I'm not sure about Raquel, though."

Margo stepped right in front of him. "Sasha has told me about Raquel's family and the troubles. You watch her, hotshot." Her emerald eyes were more serious than Cole had ever seen them. "You make sure nothing happens to her."

"I'll watch her, Red."

She narrowed her eyes. "When you bring Raquel back, you and I will have words over that nickname."

He evaded her gaze, didn't answer.

But the woman was sharp. She drew in a breath, her tone accusing. "I would not have pegged you as a coward. You intend to break her heart."

He shoved his hands deep in his pockets, clenched his jaw. "I don't intend a damn thing. Did it ever occur to you she might just break mine?"

"Never if she can help it."

Cole had trouble holding the other woman's censuring gaze. His poker face was damned rusty and Margo St-Pierre knew how to call a bluff.

"I'll send her back, Margo, as soon as it's safe."

"But you will not return." It wasn't a question.

Cole looked up at the clear sky that held no traces of the storm that had moved through just last night. He wanted to believe that Raquel would be fine on her own, without him. Still, he worried. "You'll be there for her?" he asked.

"*Oui*, hotshot. A friend to me is one for life."

He nodded, ignoring the barb he knew was woven through her words. These people would not treat Raquel differently. "She's lucky to have you."

"But she wants *you*. And I do not think I am so far off the mark in believing that you feel the same for her. I have seen how you watch her with your heart."

"Where Raquel's safety is concerned, I can't afford to have a heart."

"Keep repeating the lie," she taunted. "Perhaps soon you will even believe it."

He was saved from answering when Raquel came out of the house. He reached for her suitcase, frowning at her outfit. The perfectly correct suit of an heiress in a shade of pink so delicate it reminded him of a dawn-kissed cloud.

For some reason, the skirt, blazer and sensible pumps made him angry. And sad. He'd gotten used to her dragging any old thing out of the closet, had even looked forward to the sexy, and at times, bohemian outfits.

Now, with the donning of the conservative clothes, came the mask.

She met his scrutiny with squared shoulders and a look so regal he wanted to shake her. The facade was up, an expression she'd spent years perfecting. But Cole knew her too well, knew the turmoil that swirled inside her over returning to Valldoria.

Uncaring that Margo looked on with smug satisfaction, he gently tipped Raquel's chin up. "You've got guts, spitfire. You don't need to hide behind clothes."

Her chest rose on a sigh. "Pitiful what a lifetime of conditioning will do to a person, isn't it?"

"There's not one thing that's pitiful about you."

She smiled at him, a smile so soft he could have sworn he heard his heart crack. With her gaze alone, she held him spellbound, and when she pressed her mouth to his, no warning in the world could have budged him. He savored her taste, the feel of her body so close.

When she stepped back, he wasn't certain his voice would work. He gave it a try anyway. "Any more bags?"

Rich auburn hair swished across the padded shoulders of her blazer as she shook her head. "I will only be away a week."

The reminder was very subtle and very gentle. Cole turned away before he could beg her for a lifetime.

Margo, eyebrow arched, met his gaze. Damn it, he hated smug women.

RAQUEL NOTICED how Cole followed her with his eyes. It was more than keeping her within his sights. Each time she looked around she met his gaze. It was a look that spoke of…love.

Yet she must be wrong, wishful thinking. He'd never indicated anything deeper.

And that was her own fault. She'd been the one to insist there would be no possessive strings to bind. She'd thought it would be enough, the lovemaking, thought she could keep it light, enjoy the relationship for whatever time they had left.

She'd been very wrong.

She needed more than ecstasy. She needed permanence. Someone there at the end of the day to give a back rub, to walk with her, to share the joys and sorrows of her day.

He couldn't be there. Couldn't be the one. And the hopelessness of that realization nearly tore her in two.

She felt his hand touch hers where it lay on the plush armrest of the Learjet. She turned her palm, linked her fingers with his and squeezed.

"You okay?" he asked softly.

"Yes. It is silly really. The closer we get to home, the more uneasy I become. My stomach is dancing as if I am in a panic."

He didn't pull his hand away, and she was grateful.

"You're a different woman who's returning, spitfire. You've got a lot to be proud of."

"I know. So why do I feel so jumpy?"

He raised their joined hands, pressed his lips to the back of hers. "It's the clothes. Stuffy and prim. They're probably sending off bad vibes and messing with your karma."

She stared at him for several seconds, then laughed and dropped her head on his shoulder. "That is the most un-Cole-like thing I have ever heard you say!"

He grinned. "Got you to smile, didn't it?"

"You are very sneaky. And very good for me." She felt a slight jolt from him. "And I only wore this outfit because I did not want to shock anyone too soon."

"Meaning you'll cut loose tomorrow?"

"You never know. Perhaps as soon as tonight."

"I don't think Dama Santiago is ready for that crochet thing that shows your bra."

"Ah, you liked that one."

"Yeah. I'm not real crazy about my Guard seeing you in it though. Or Prince Joseph. He'll be regretting what he missed out on."

She laughed again. "There is little danger of that. He has his perfect princess."

"Will you visit with Briana while you're here?"

While you're here. Just that quickly, laughter fled, making her feel as though a bowling ball had rolled a strike to her stomach. The reminder that her time with Cole was limited. "I would love to see Briana."

His fingers tightened around hers. "I hate to bring up sore subjects, but the rules will be status quo. No going out unattended. Not until we get to the bottom of the unrest."

She glanced at him. "I should not have cut my hair."

"What does that have to do with anything?"

"If I start to feel trapped, I was thinking I could let down my hair and you could climb to my rescue."

"Nobody's locking you in a tower, Raquel."

"It will feel as such. I have gotten used to coming and going as I please."

"You can still do that. You'll just have an escort."

"Then nothing has really changed—other than the fact that I am no longer expected to marry the prince. I will have no privacy. Unless of course, that escort will be you?"

"I'll be around," he evaded. "But don't count on me. I'll be busy."

"I am the last one who will want to interfere with your work, Cole. My father's life could be at stake—"

"Or yours."

She ignored the interruption. "But you will not be required to work around the clock. Promise me you will make the time for us."

"Raquel, it's not a good idea to... It would be best if no one knew of our intimacy."

She licked her lips, saw his blue eyes flare.

"Don't start," he warned.

"You know, there are times when I am certain I could hit you. You are forever creating obstacles—my virginity...your honor. I say the devil take it all. Must I begin the seduction all over again?"

"Ah, hell."

"Kiss me, Cole."

He shook his head. "The crew could come back here any minute."

"So?"

"So, they're employed by your father. You know how fast gossip spreads."

"Let them gossip. I am no longer betrothed. I am free to have a relationship with a man."

"Not with the hired help."

"The urge to hit you is getting much much stronger." This man was as far from hired help as one could get. He had too much...presence. She put her hand on his thigh, inching her palm upward. "However, I would much rather make love than war."

"Woman, you're killing me."

"Then stop fighting."

It was doubtful that the crew would disturb them—he'd only been grabbing at thin excuses. So Cole gave in to what his heart and body ached for. Cursing the armrest separating them, he jerked it upward and took her in his arms.

The scent of wildflowers surrounded him. He savored

her lips, storing the memories. One week was too short. So he poured all the longing he felt into that single kiss, hoping it would be enough, knowing it wouldn't.

He loved the way she flowed into him, met him more than halfway, gave as good as she got. He loved the feel of her smooth skin, her smoky voice, her exotic eyes, her gentleness with babies. He loved her lips and her taste.

And by God, he was getting carried away.

Drawing back, he tucked a strand of hair behind her ear. "We're steaming up the windows of the jet."

"Can't have that." Her voice was breathy, aroused. "The pilot will crash us."

"Bite your tongue."

"I would much rather you do that for me."

Man alive, he went from hard to rigid in less than a second. If he didn't cool down he wouldn't be able to stand. "Have a care for the fogged windows, spitfire."

She gave his face a gentle stroke, then leaned away. She could feel the Learjet making its descent. The pilot's voice came over the speaker system.

"We will be landing in approximately six minutes, Mr. Martinez. I ask that you fasten your seat belt, Miss Santiago."

Raquel reached for the belt as Cole lowered the armrest. "Are you exempt from safety harnesses?" she asked. The pilot had only told *her* to belt up.

Cole stood. "I'll be up front for the landing, monitoring the radio and such."

"Ah, doing your thing. I can see that you're dying to get at it." She grinned and shook her head. "Really, Cole, I understand your love of gadgets. You did not have to stay back here with me."

He bent down and brushed his lips against hers. "The

scenery's much better back here. And you win hands down over gadgets any day, spitfire.''

"Flatterer. Go.''

Buckled in, she leaned over and glanced out the window. Below them she could see the verdant landscape of Valldoria.

Her country.

There was nothing prisonlike about it. Beautiful waterfalls flowed into serene grottoes. Stately oaks shaded the banks of the lakes, where people enjoyed water sports. The homes were spacious and occupied good-size plots, so neighbors were not on top of one another.

As they banked for landing she saw the harbor, her family's main source of wealth. All import and export of platinum and other goods came through this harbor. Transportation was the Santiago business. Shipping by sea, by rail, by truck or by air. They controlled it all.

Raquel admitted that she *did* love this land and its people. What she couldn't abide were the restrictions that came with being who she was—an heiress, who for twenty-five years had been expected to be both princess and future queen.

Everyone knew her face and her name. And along with that recognition came responsibilities. Responsibilities she no longer wished to cater to. She'd had a taste of freedom, reveled in it, knew she'd wilt like a pansy in the Sahara if she lost that coveted freedom.

And she would wilt if she stayed. Here in Valldoria she could not be anonymous, would be trailed by an entourage if she simply took a walk in the gardens to pick flowers.

She would be watched…and judged. The Santiagos were not unlike the royal family—and the citizens of

Valldoria loved their celebrities, felt it their God-given right to judge, censure and gossip about them.

Still, no matter how nasty the gossip or accusations, when it came down to it, Valldorians would remain fiercely loyal and continue to love.

Which was why Raquel wasn't too concerned over people's opinions with regard to her jilting Prince Joseph. They would forgive her. Especially since Joseph had gotten his happy ending with Briana.

And that brought to mind another matter that worried her. What if her family and the people were determined for *her* to have a happy ending, too?

Her stomach lurched and she knew it wasn't from the aircraft's descent.

She would not have a happily-ever-after. Because she would be returning to France as soon as the danger to her father passed. She had a deadline to meet, a business to run, a life of freedom and independence.

And when she left, Cole would not be coming with her. She knew that for certain.

A stinging sensation roiled in her stomach again. Leaving Cole would be like leaving a piece of herself behind, like ripping open a wound that would never heal.

She felt the tears back up in her throat, felt the horrible ache of loss before it even happened.

Their days together this week would be bittersweet. They would have to make the most of them. To pack a lifetime of sweet memories into a few short days.

"I'D ALMOST FORGOTTEN about all the ceremony," Raquel said as the motorcade passed through the gates of the Santiago estate.

Cole, sitting across from her in the limo, glanced out

the window. "I called ahead to let them know we were coming in."

"I suppose I should feel honored. I am no longer a princess in waiting, yet I can see that a good portion of the Royal Guard is present."

He hadn't told her about the photo tacked to her door, or its message. "You're an important woman, spitfire."

She winced. "But I only want to be ordinary. A photographer who cuddles babies."

Just looking at her, no one would consider her ordinary. The regal bearing was as much a part of her as her skin. "I never thought I'd say this, but I'll miss those kids."

She smiled softly, and leaned forward to touch his knee, her exotic brown eyes hopeful. "There are still the weekends. You know Papa will let you use the jet."

He couldn't hold her gaze because it hurt too much. Hurt to think about what he'd had for only a few days. Hurt to know that it couldn't continue. Anything short of marriage would put both his job and her reputation in jeopardy.

Yet marriage was not an option. Because of who she'd become, Raquel couldn't stay. And because of who he was, he couldn't go. And to dally outside the bounds of marriage with her was out of the question. Her family took their position and beliefs seriously. They were devout Catholics and would not tolerate the sin.

A sin that would ruin both her reputation and his job.

"Let's get through this crisis first." He hated to evade, knew he'd have to gently ease back. Dealing with the unrest would help; it would give him something to occupy his time.

It was the nights that would be a killer. The endless

stretch of darkness where thoughts and images would haunt him.

Raquel curled her fingers into her palm as the limousine stopped in front of the estate. She could see the lie in Cole's eyes, knew that her hope rested on shaky ground.

He wouldn't be visiting her on the weekends. When she left, it would be a final goodbye.

She got a grip on her melancholy thoughts as one of the sentries pulled open the limo's door. The climate-controlled interior of the car immediately went up several degrees as hot, dry air swirled in.

"Stay put for a sec," Cole said. He got out of the car, accepted a portable radio and spoke into it. Then he turned and reached out a hand to help her out of the car.

"Welcome home, Senorita Santiago." His words were spoken formally, but the reassuring squeeze of his fingers was not.

"I hope all this fuss is not for me." The Valldorian guards stood at attention in perfect formation, like a human barricade, creating an aisleway to the massive front doors of the estate.

"Some of it's for you. We've borrowed several units from the palace. In addition to your father's own security, my men have been in place to make sure that no one gets past."

Raquel was used to the sight of the Guard. Still the oppression weighed her down, smothering her. She felt on display, hemmed in. She told herself to march right through that human pathway, to ignore the panic that clawed at her, to forget about the memories of a lonely childhood, the images of Rapunzel trapped in the tower.

Guarded. Watched...trapped.

She wanted to slip her hand in Cole's, yet she could already feel his distance, his formal diplomacy in the presence of watchful eyes.

Dios, she hated the idea of correctness, of protocol. She was no longer a young girl. She was a woman with a spine and she would face her family in that manner.

Impulsively, she peeled off her blazer. The September heat did not warrant a jacket. And she was just off balance enough to want to flaunt convention lest it suck her back in. The cropped, clingy tank top exposed her midriff.

Cole glanced at her sharply. There was surprise there…and admiration…and desire.

She met his gaze, chin lifted, daring him to forget himself. Just for the moment.

"Most people gain confidence from donning clothes. Yours seems to skyrocket when you take them off."

"I had an instructor once who told me, 'Start as you mean to go on.'"

"And you mean to shock a few people."

"Is being who I am so shocking?"

"Ah, no, spitfire." He almost reached out to touch her. She saw his arm lift then drop to his side, his fingers curled into a fist as if to keep them from straying.

It would be an uphill battle to break through the barriers he'd erected again.

And it suddenly became very important that she do just that. They only had a week. And she intended to store more memories in that week. Many more.

"You hesitate to touch me, yet I see your desire," she said softly, taking care that her voice did not carry to interested ears. "In public, I will let you get away with it. In private will be a different matter. I will not let you avoid me."

Without giving him a chance to respond, she squared her shoulders and started up the pathway. Like life-size toy soldiers, the men stood at attention, expressionless in their black-and-gold uniforms, rifles held rigidly with the barrels pointing upward. Helmets resembling over-size construction hard hats covered their heads, dipping nearly to the men's noses, their eyes barely visible.

"You know, I could use one of those helmets as a prop for the babies. What do you think, Cole?"

His lips quirked. "A baby soldier or a kid in a spittoon might not go over too well with the public."

She laughed. "Oh, you are right. They do look a bit like a spittoon upended. I've always thought someone made a mistake in the sizing of the things. They look entirely too large." She stopped in front of one of the men, peering into his eyes. His stoic expression slipped when he got a good look at her, especially up this close.

Cole gently took her elbow. These men were highly trained. In formation, they never gave away any emotions. Yet he'd seen several of the Guard fail in that respect as Raquel passed. No doubt her new hairstyle and the sexy tank top hugging her breasts and exposing her waist raised figurative eyebrows.

Covertly, Cole watched the men and knew that it was more than the exterior appearance the soldiers were dying to respond to. It was Raquel's carriage, the self-assurance that surrounded her like an aura of mystery. Enticing.

But Cole knew her well, knew that she clawed for that self-assurance with every ounce of her energy.

The massive front doors opened. Carlos and Pilar Santiago stood there, smiles of welcome for their prodigal daughter.

Cole ushered Raquel inside, closing the door behind them.

"You are home at last," Pilar exclaimed, then sucked in a breath. "Your hair! Where are your beautiful long tresses?"

"On the floor of a beauty shop in France."

"But why? And the color—the red streaks. *Madre de Dios,* Raquel. The Santiagos do *not* have red hair!"

"This Santiago does."

Cole saw Raquel's forced smile. When she turned to look at him, he detected a note of panic in her eyes. Yet he couldn't go to her, couldn't take her in his arms and promise her it would be okay.

He didn't have the right to promise her anything.

Raquel felt her heart sink when Cole turned away from her. It was as if her lifeline was slipping away.

And these wimpy emotions were pitiful. This was her family, for crying out loud.

"Well," Pilar said. "Our hairdresser can set things right. The important thing is that you are home."

"Yes, Mama, I am home…for now."

"What is this 'for now'? We have much to do, much to catch up on. Where are your bags? Oh, never mind," she answered herself. "Your room is just as you left it. With the closets full." Pilar Santiago's gaze was somewhat scandalized as she took in Raquel's bare stomach.

No doubt her mother was picturing the contents of the upstairs wardrobe for a more suitable outfit.

Three closets, Raquel remembered. She suddenly wanted to run out to the limo and retrieve the suitcase she'd brought. The clothes waiting upstairs would feel foreign. She wanted her leggings and sloppy man-style shirts, her jeans, her hip-hugger pants and crop tops.

Looking at her beautiful mother, Raquel noticed the

strain around her eyes and felt small for worrying about herself when there were threats surrounding this family.

They'd never been a demonstrative family. Even now, the extent of touching was the linking of both hands. Raquel let go of her mother's hands and enveloped her in a hug.

"Oh, Mama, I see your worry. I should have come sooner."

Pilar was surprised and stiff for a moment. Then she awkwardly returned the hug. "We are well protected, and you are here now."

Raquel leaned back, searching her mother's smooth features. "You are fine?"

"Of course."

She turned, meeting Carlos Santiago's gaze. A head shorter than Cole, her father still emanated an aura of power that garnered respect. There, too, was worry. A worry he hid well.

"Hello, daughter."

Raquel grinned and treated him to the same show of affection, wrapping her arms around his tough frame. "So you are creating enemies in my absence, Papa?"

"Nothing for you to worry about, girl."

"But I do worry, Papa."

He patted her shoulder and stepped back. Physical displays were not his style. "Never know it with you running off like some commoner. You forget who you are. And where is the rest of your blouse? It is unseemly to dress so."

Two strikes, she thought. First the hair, now the clothes. Then again, she'd expected as much.

Her cheeks ached from the strain of keeping her smile in place. She gestured to the jacket draped over her arm. "I assure you I was well covered in public."

"Well..." He seemed ill at ease, at a loss for words. Which wasn't like the dynamic man she'd known all her life. "Your mother will see to your wardrobe."

He turned to Cole, already dismissing her. "I have set up a command room just as you asked. Your man, Cruz, is there now. Come, I'll take you there."

Although her feelings stung from the abrupt dismissal, Raquel wanted to know what was going on.

She wanted to know where Cole would be.

"Will Cole be staying at the estate, Papa?"

Santiago halted and glanced at his daughter with a frown. Behind him, Cole's eyes telegraphed a warning. She shot the look right back at him. If he was going to insist that they sneak to see one another, she at least wanted to know where and how far she needed to skulk.

"I am here because there was an attempt on your life, Papa. I want to be kept abreast of what is going on."

"This is not a matter you should worry about."

"But I am worried. And you are, too, otherwise you would not have sent Cole to guard me."

"He was sent to bring you home. Well over a week ago," he stressed, an underlying censure in his tone he didn't bother to hide.

"I could not come a week ago. I have a business to run." She dared him to call her business a hobby.

He refrained.

"Follow us if you must, Raquel." Carlos turned on his heel, obviously assuming she and Cole would follow. And why wouldn't they? Rarely did one disobey her father's orders.

To Cole he said, "We have taken several rooms off the kitchen and outfitted them as a surveillance office. King Marcos is still cooperating, and you are on loan to us. So I have taken the liberty of having the rooms next to the command post turned into a guest suite.''

Carlos glanced at his daughter with a look that seemed to say, Did that answer your question?

Raquel dared to give her father a saucy look. *Dios!* If she didn't know better, she'd think he was still miffed that she'd jilted the royal prince.

She nearly grinned when her gaze collided with Cole's. Standing behind her father, his blue eyes were alight with amused indulgence.

She felt encouraged, and proud of herself for the small acts of defiance. Never before would she have dreamed of giving her father such a look—or demanding answers.

But she'd gotten the information she'd been after.

She and Cole would still be residing under the same roof. And that knowledge made the coming week seem a little brighter.

Chapter Thirteen

Raquel felt a sense of déjà vu as she sat in the cushioned window seat of her bedroom, staring down at the grounds below. Cole stood just beyond the portico, conferring with Johnny Cruz.

He was avoiding her. That much was obvious. Oh, she knew he had security business to attend to, but they hadn't spoken in the last twenty-four hours.

As though he felt the weight of her stare, he looked up. Their gazes locked and held. Her heart sped up and her fingers trembled as she rested them against the glass panes.

She saw his shoulders stiffen, imagined that she saw regret in his eyes. A lump formed in her throat when he turned away.

It wouldn't be the first time her imagination had run away with her. If he regretted not being with her, then surely he'd make the effort to engineer a meeting. She certainly had. To no avail.

Each time she sought him out, she ran into Johnny Cruz instead. What good was it to have Cole under the same roof if the man wouldn't stay put?

It appeared that the sweet memories she'd planned to hoard this week would never materialize. He was acting as though she'd already left, as though what they'd shared in France had never been.

Feeling uptight over having nothing to do—and nobody to do it with—Raquel wandered downstairs and poured a cup of coffee from the silver pot on the sideboard. She missed waking up with the expectation of the babies, of their sweet faces, of capturing those wonderful expressions on film.

And she missed Cole.

Sitting down, she propped her elbow on the dining table and toyed with her coffee.

Pilar breezed in, a cloud of Chanel No. 5 wafting in her wake.

"Good. You are up," Pilar said. After pouring herself a cup of coffee and adding a dollop of cream she joined Raquel and instantly launched into all the functions scheduled in the coming weeks.

"Really, Raquel, we must have the seamstress visit. Your choice of clothing is hardly fit for gardening."

Raquel glanced down at her sleeveless shell and pencil-slim, figure-hugging pants. She'd seen a Paris runway model wearing the same outfit.

Unable to work up any enthusiasm for a comeback, Raquel merely shrugged.

"I am so pleased you are here to join me in the many invitations that are pouring in—"

"You mean you're not under house arrest?"

Pilar frowned at the interruption but kept her poise. "It is nasty business, this unrest…and in such a peaceful community. But duty must prevail. A rotten apple cannot spoil what is expected of the Santiagos. Your papa understands this and I am well guarded when I go out. The security will extend to you as well."

"Naturally," Raquel muttered.

Pilar folded her hands in her lap. "It is wonderful that you are home, my daughter. Now, more than ever, we must present a united front."

Raquel only half listened. In her mind's eye she kept picturing Cole in her rocking chair in France, cradling a sleepy infant.

"Did you hear me, *mi hija?*"

"Mama, I am not staying," she said absently, by rote.

"Nonsense. You are home. We must catch up—"

"Have there been new babies born since I've been gone?"

Pilar stared, mouth agape, inspecting Raquel as though aliens had invaded the body of her beloved child. "Well, uh...Constanza Esparta had a beautiful set of twins and—"

"Twins?" Her spirits lifted. "Oh, I must see them."

"But of course. The garden society luncheon I mentioned will be at the Esparta home and..." Her words trailed off and her perfectly made-up eyes widened as if a light had dawned. "Ah, my sweet, you are wanting to photograph the babies in the gardens?"

Raquel's mind was already busy with ideas. "I brought my cameras. I can improvise on the props—no fancy costumes, just simple flower wreaths straight from the grounds."

Yes, it could be done, she thought. Valldoria was a beautiful land, a world painted with a deep, rich palette, burnished by a gentle sun, where meadows of gold and lavender stretched for miles.

A perfect backdrop for a baby wreathed in flowers.

"Oh dear, I do not think your father would approve." The softly spoken words held the barest hint of censure. Not exactly a wet blanket, but a damp one none-theless.

"Mama, photographing babies is what I do now. I would appreciate your support."

Pilar wrung her hands, so very unlike the powerful, poised woman. "You have no need to work. Your papa has provided so well for you."

"Please, do not let us disagree, *Madre*. When I leave this time, I would like for it to be on better terms."

"No!"

"Yes," Raquel said gently. "I like providing for my-self. I love my job. I must go back."

LATE THAT NIGHT, when the estate was quiet, Raquel made her way to the computer room. Although he hadn't issued an invitation, she set aside her pride and went to him, disliking that it had to be under the cover of darkness, when the rest of the household slept.

Hesitating in the doorway, she glanced around the room. Security monitors flanked the walls, silent elec-tronic eyes guarding the grounds. Cole sat in front of a fax machine, reading a document, the monitor of his computer casting a green glow in the dim, artificial light of the room.

She hadn't made a sound, yet he turned, his blue eyes flaring for a bare instant as though she were his sun and moon and stars all wrapped together with a gossamer bow.

Her heart responded to that look with a glad leap. Then as if her eyes had deceived her, his expression went curiously blank, retreating behind a veil of polite-ness.

Politeness, for crying out loud. As though they had not made passionate love just two nights ago.

Raquel almost whirled around and left. But something kept her there, a force that was stronger than she could fight.

Was it so selfish of her to want these days with him? People had casual affairs all the time and went their separate ways. Why not them?

The problem was, this didn't feel casual.

And her need to touch him overpowered all else.

She moved into the room. "You look tired. When is your relief due?"

"Any time now."

Smoothing her palms over his shoulders, she kneaded his tense muscles.

After a minute he relaxed. "Mmm. That feels good. How're you doing, spitfire?"

"I miss the babies." *And I miss you.* "Are you making any headway?" She nodded toward the files spread before him.

"Speculation only. Nothing that I can act on."

"Who is at the top of your list?"

He reached for her hands, drew her around and pulled her onto his lap. Assured of privacy, he couldn't resist holding her, drinking in her wildflower essence. "Sure you want to talk about business?"

She pressed her lips to his neck, rested her head on his shoulder. She filled his arms and his heart, made him ache for what he couldn't have.

Or, more accurately, what he couldn't hold.

"There are much better things I would rather do with you," she said, her breath warm against his neck, "but you are on duty and you look like you could use a good sounding board. Perhaps another mind will spark a detail you have overlooked."

"I rarely overlook details, spitfire." He felt the smile

work its way from his heart to his lips. He could spend the rest of his life, just like this, with Raquel wrapped in his arms. "You got a yen to do some detective work?"

"There's not much else to do around here. I've gotten out of the habit of being a prissy lady. Besides, we made a pretty good team with the babies. I will return the favor and become your assistant. Heaven knows, my mind could use some stimulation."

"Only your mind?" He was turning into a first-class masochist.

Her hand crept up his shirtfront, toying with the loosened knot of his tie. "Other parts, too, but first I'd like an update on your progress, who you think sent the letter bomb."

He reached around her and opened a file, spreading out photos and vital statistics and background information.

"Recognize this guy?"

She leaned forward, shifting in his lap, making him burn.

"No. Should I?"

"Probably not. His name's Rafael Cordoba. He was the chief financial officer of Santiago shipping."

"Was?"

"Mmm. Your father fired him last month. Caught him with his fingers in the till."

"Skimming? Did Papa not pay him a good salary?"

"He paid him damned well. Cordoba got greedy."

"Well, it seems open and shut to me. Obviously this man is angry and out for retaliation. Why don't you just arrest him and be done with it?"

"I don't have anything concrete to charge him with."

"But you think he is involved?"

His fingers tightened around her hip. With her on his lap, her sweet butt cradled against him, he found it was damned hard to concentrate.

"According to the dossier we've compiled, the guy's got a background in explosives. He'd have the knowledge to rig a bomb."

She twisted around to look at him, her expressive brown eyes serious. "You must conduct a search of his premises, I think. Have you done so?"

Cole grinned. "Want to join my Guard, spitfire?"

Her eyes narrowed playfully. "I could probably run circles around your men."

"You probably could." He swept a strand of hair behind her ear. "And to answer your question, yes, we went in with a search warrant."

"And?"

"Nothing turned up. No sign of explosives."

"Perhaps he has a secret hideaway."

He loved the way she went all serious on him, the way her hand rested on his chest, just above his heart. "You're dangerous."

"I try. Was anyone else involved? An accomplice? Or did he act alone in the skimming?"

"A couple of dock workers went down with him." He lifted another file. "Maurice Patillas. He's what we call a planner. His position is to organize the loading of ships, mostly by computer. He knows where everything is by weight and size, makes sure the ship won't leave port unbalanced and get capsized by a rogue wave."

"And knowing this, he can easily steal bits and pieces of the cargo," she said, nodding thoughtfully.

"Seems that's what he's been up to. He's a quiet guy,

lives simply. He accepted his dismissal without argument and refused to name names."

"As opposed to Rafael Cordoba?"

"Right. Cordoba's blaming everybody but himself, claiming he was a victim. He's pointing the finger at Phil Dominguez. Forklift driver."

"Which of the men has the most to lose?"

"Depends on how you look at it. Cordoba's screaming the loudest, making threats. Being a top executive, he's accustomed to a certain life-style. The other two live lower- to middle-class. In any of the cases, loss of job and wages will have an impact."

"What does your gut tell you?"

"I'm not inclined to trust gut instincts." He tossed the file back on the workstation.

Raquel's gaze followed the sailing missive. It landed off-center, upsetting a neat stack of papers.

Everything within her system stilled, went on alert. Slowly, she scooted off his lap and stood, reaching for a photograph that had been uncovered.

An eight-by-ten glossy of Cole.

Her easy mood vanished. Feeling shaky and confused, she stared at the image, the one she'd taken in France.

The one that had been stolen.

The blood in her veins turned to ice as she read the single word scrawled in big red letters.

Boom.

"I hadn't meant for you to see that," Cole said, his voice filled with both disgust and apology.

She turned slowly, looked at him, feeling betrayed. "Why?"

"Because you'd worry." He tried to take the photo, but she held it back. "It's my job to do the worrying."

"Do you know how angry a comment like that makes me?" she asked very softly, very carefully. "I was shielded most of my life. Now I am thrown back into my parents' home, back to where I clawed to get away from. I am holding on by a thread to keep from falling back into my old patterns...I thought you of all people would give me more credit, treat me with more respect, like an intelligent woman who can do more than attend silly teas and worry over the correct clothes."

She stopped, took a breath, her words a mere whisper now. "I expected more from you, Cole. I counted on you to understand."

"I do."

He reached for her but she stepped away. If he touched her now, she'd crumble.

"Do you? And when were you going to tell me that in addition to my father's life being in jeopardy, some creep was also gunning for you? From your casket, perhaps?"

"There's no need to overreact—"

"Don't you dare accuse me of melodrama!" she snapped. Dragging a hand through her hair, she paced away from him. "I've had it up to here with overprotective males." She made a slicing gesture in the area of her forehead. "Did you think I was too weak or too stupid to handle this...this warning?"

She shook the photo at him, fury all but blinding her. "I slept with you. And I don't do that sort of thing lightly." Words tumbled out now without caution. "The hell with you, Cole Martinez. There may be no strings of commitment to bind us, but I care. I would not be just some empty-headed heiress attending your funeral. I would be..." The words *the woman who loves you* remained choked in her throat.

This time he didn't let her whirl away from him. He snatched her to him, held her close, his arms like gentle, loving bands around her. "I apologize."

She started to yell at him. Then she saw his eyes, saw that he was not merely placating her. She saw what he held back with such rigid control. Fear.

Fear for her, for them, for the events that were out of his control.

Accusations melted away. She touched his face, held his gaze, allowed her own emotions to show.

Her love.

"And well you should be," she said softly, pressing her lips to his jaw, then stepping out of his arms. Unless the man was blind, he'd understood what her eyes had silently told him. She didn't want to push the issue, because she still didn't have a solution...a solution for their future.

"Where did this come from?" She held up the photo, her steady look fairly daring him to evade her questions, to couch them in cotton.

It was a long moment before he dragged his gaze away from hers. "I found it tacked to your front door the morning we got the call from Valldoria."

She looked back at the photo. "So now you know for certain you are dealing with more than one man."

"Not necessarily. Our perp could have flown to France and been back in time to deliver the bomb."

"You are smart, Cole. I imagine you have already checked the round-trip tickets issued on those days."

"There's always private flights."

"You really should take me on as your assistant. There is a very important clue you are missing."

His mouth canted slightly. "What's that?"

"This photograph is a copy."

His features went from relaxed to rigid in a flash. "Are you sure?"

"Of course I am sure. I do my own processing on a special paper I order from Paris. This is not printed on my stock."

He took the photo, turned it over. "Can it be traced? Do you know which lab uses this paper?"

She shrugged. "It is generic, used worldwide. To trace it would be like searching for a pinhead in a platinum mine. Just about every photo lab in France, here and in the States could use this brand."

Cole swore. The damned thing had been missing for two days. Add another thirty-six hours for the time they'd been in Valldoria and that equaled a trail gone stone-cold.

"What next?" Raquel asked, the soft touch of her fingertips on his cheek bringing him out of his inward disgust.

He looked into her eyes, eyes that telegraphed an emotion he recognized, an emotion that scared the hell out of him.

Not now! he wanted to shout. *I'm not the right man.*

"Next, we fire up every computer at our disposal and burn up the phone lines looking for the pinhead in the platinum mine."

And run down Lucian Delgado, he added silently. The coincidence of the pretty boy's timing was too suspicious to ignore.

A coincidence he berated himself for not thinking of sooner.

A shadow on the monitor drew his gaze and Cole stepped back, moving across the room.

Johnny Cruz appeared in the doorway, glancing at

Raquel, then at Cole. He nodded at Raquel. "Senorita Santiago. I see you've made contact at last."

It upset her that Cole had abruptly created physical as well as emotional distance, that he was so careful to make sure no one suspected what was between them.

Forcing a lightness to her tone, she responded to Cruz's observation. "Yes, I have run him to ground so to speak. And please, call me Raquel. I have interrupted you so many times today, we can surely be considered old friends."

Cruz's smile was very slight, his nod almost imperceptible as he looked toward Cole for orders.

Raquel noticed that Cole was frowning.

"There is no need to scowl at the man, Cole. As I told my father, I have a stake in this investigation. I wanted to be kept abreast of the progress. Johnny, however, has been properly tight-lipped, referring me to you for answers."

She felt ridiculous, pretending this was only an innocent visit, especially since the emotions in the room were probably still thick enough to cut with a machete.

Cole nodded, then went into a figurative huddle with his relief man, apprising Cruz of the latest developments.

Dios! By the look on his face one would think he believed she'd been having a secret rendezvous with Johnny Cruz.

Raquel could have slipped out of the room, but she knew Cole was officially off duty now that Johnny was here.

That meant he would have time for her. Private time. And though she figured he'd balk at the possibility of being caught, she intended to push for that time.

After a few minutes, he looked up, his preoccupied

gaze clearly telling her he'd forgotten she was in the room.

That piqued her ego, and she sent him a look hot enough to sizzle.

He tugged at his tie. "I will escort Miss Santiago back to her quarters. Call if you need anything."

Smothering a smile, Raquel followed him out of the room.

"Pretty gutsy," she teased. "With the house secure, there is little danger of me being accosted in my own hallway. Are you not worried that Johnny will be suspicious?"

Cole took her elbow to hurry her along. The sassy woman had him tied in knots. And that sultry look had nearly fried his brain—an occurrence that was becoming entirely too frequent. "Cruz is a good man. He's discreet."

"Mmm. *Bueno.* So will you show me your temporary quarters now?"

"Not *that* discreet."

"Do not be stuffy. I am perfectly willing to see you openly. You are the one who insists on sneaking. To that end, should anyone inquire as to why I am in your bedroom, we will simply tell them I am inspecting its comfort standards. After all, the Santiagos are traditionally hospitable to their guests."

"I won't disrespect Don Carlos under his own roof, Raquel."

"Fine, then, we'll go to your house."

He pulled her to a halt at the bottom of the winding staircase, turning her to face him. To the right of them was the front door. It was tempting to usher her out into the night, to take her to his house, to his bed.

But he couldn't. This had to stop. Prolonging the relationship was only torturing them both.

"Cole?" Where moments ago her voice had been light and teasing, now it held a slight tremble. "I do not like that look that has come over your face. I have seen it too many times, the times when you are intent on running from me."

He closed his eyes. "Don't you see? I've screwed up enough as it is. Someone breached the alarm right under my nose in France. That photo showed up. And why?"

He tried to keep his voice down, tried to ignore the bruised look that shadowed her eyes. "It happened because I was preoccupied with my emotions, my feelings for you. I can't gamble with your life that way, Raquel. I won't."

"You are being much too hard on yourself. You cannot be everywhere at once."

"No, but I can focus my concentration. I can't do that around you. Because the minute I lay eyes on you, all I want to do is find a way to convince you to stay." He hadn't meant to say that, could have flayed himself alive when he saw the tenuous hope in her eyes. He shook his head. "And that would be really stupid."

"Maybe—"

"Don't," he interrupted sharply. Softly now. "Don't. I see how this place sucks the life out of you."

She started to shake her head.

He lifted her chin with a gentle finger. "You forget, I knew you before. I saw the woman you were, and I saw the woman you became in France, a woman full of life and sass. All that zest gets smothered here. I won't do that to you, spitfire. I can't."

He touched her face, broke her heart with the raw pain in his eyes, a pain that matched her own.

"You are ending our relationship, aren't you?" she whispered.

"You knew it would end."

"Not this soon."

"You can make it the rest of the week, spitfire. You'll be fine. If you need to do anything, go anywhere, Johnny will be there for you."

"I don't want Johnny. I want you." Oh, she'd known they'd eventually part. But she wasn't ready. She wanted to beg, to cling. Her throat ached, yet she refused to cry.

"I've got a job to do."

She nodded, somehow found the strength to square her shoulders. She would not stand in the way of his work. She, more than anyone, knew what it meant to be supported in a dream, in a goal. Cole's dream was the Royal Guard.

And because of her, he was beginning to doubt himself.

Her throat ached, but she managed to get words past. "I would ask one last favor."

"Anything."

"Before you close the door on us, make love to me one last time."

"Raquel—"

She covered his lips with trembling fingers, knowing she'd never survive if he rejected her now. "Once more, Cole, before you leave my life. You are off duty, there will be no jeopardy created. Give me that sweet memory. No words, just touch…then let me go."

Cole's heart thundered in his chest. If he gave in, would he give too much of his soul away? Would she feel it, know it?

He had to take the chance. Once more. And because

he wanted her, wanted those same sweet memories more than he wanted air to breathe, he gave in.

Gently, he took her hand, kissed her knuckles and walked with her up the winding staircase, even though it broke every code of honor he possessed.

He'd sell his soul and his honor for one last touch, one last taste, a memory that would have to last him a lifetime.

Her room was in an opposite wing from her parents'. Isolated.

He glanced at the window seat where he'd so often seen her sitting, the place where she'd dreamed of knights and freedom.

If the panes of those windows could talk, they'd have plenty to say. His gut twisted with an ache so sharp it was a wonder he didn't double over. This woman deserved to be the princess—not the lonely one locked away in the tower, but a beautiful, carefree, liberated princess.

"I saw you this morning." His low, deep words stirred the hair at her temple. "In the window."

"I know," she said softly. "It hurt when you turned away."

He closed his eyes, drew her close and held her as if he'd never let go, as if there were no tomorrow. "It hurt to see you there."

His lips sketched her brow, her eyelids and at last her lips. It was a kiss that said so much, and not nearly enough. "Are you sure this is what you want?"

"Yes," she whispered against his mouth. "Love me, Cole."

And he did. Slowly, reverently, silently, the mood too fragile for words to intrude, the tears too close to the surface. It was a time to hold and be held, a time to pack a lifetime of memories into a few stolen moments, moments that were too precious to miss.

There was no urgency to rush—only to savor—as he undressed her, then himself, and laid her against the brocade comforter of the raised four-poster bed.

His fingertips were like butterfly wings against her hot skin, dancing, skimming, relearning every curve and dip, every point of pleasure that only he had ever found, that only he had ever awakened.

Dear heaven, she loved the way he touched her, the way he reached for her, held her as though she were so very cherished...so loved.

How would she ever let him go? A sob built in her chest, the pain of her emotions making the sensations of pleasure sharper, so incredibly bittersweet, so precious.

With eyes open and gazes locked he eased into her. So slowly. So right. There were no second thoughts, no explanations, no questions over the past or promises for the future. Just two souls merging in a heartbreaking dance, two hearts whispering what voices dared not speak.

A gentle, utterly exquisite journey of body and soul. She saw the emotions in his eyes that he wouldn't utter, knew he could read the same in hers.

Emotions so powerful she wanted to weep.

The electrifying beauty of their joining was stunning. She felt him deep inside her, felt him throb, felt her own body pick up the rhythm, respond in kind. Her fingers curled into his shoulders, asking for more. So much more.

Where before she'd reveled in the quiet solace, now the urgency built. He understood her need as if he'd read her mind.

And he gave it. Slowly at first, then with building speed, the friction of his thrust like a loving chant, a chant that would echo in her soul and heart until the day she died.

Gazes still locked, breath mingling, he took her to the edge of forever…and incredibly, beyond even the farthest flaming star.

With a strength born of sorrow, of fear, of the horrible sadness of a love that would never see the open light of day, she held him tight, holding on until the last tremor had subsided, until her breath was steady and their bodies were no longer damp.

And though it felt as if her heart would split in two, she forced herself to honor her promise to let him go.

Sitting up, she reached for her robe, knowing he'd take his cue from her actions.

The mattress shifted and she closed her eyes. She couldn't bear to watch him dress, so she kept her back turned lest she betray them both and beg him to stay.

Steady, she cautioned herself when the silence in the room told her he was dressed. Waiting.

Her eyes stung, but she ignored the pain and stood to face him. The ends of his tie hung loose around his neck. His vivid blue eyes were filled with regret, and something so much deeper, a raw emotion that matched her own flayed spirit.

She saw his lips part, knew he was about to speak, knew that if he did she'd lose her nerve.

She shook her head, leaned forward and pressed her mouth to his. With her touch alone, she told him she loved him….

Told him goodbye.

When he drew back, she saw his Adam's apple bob,

felt the tremor in his fingertips as he mapped her features, held her gaze for a heartbeat more.

"Take care of yourself," she whispered.

He nodded, then turned and left the room.

Left her life.

Holding on to her emotions by a mere thread, she moved to the window seat, looking out at the night. The sky was a deep lapis blue, brightened only by a sprinkling of stars and the moonglow that streamed through the beveled panes of her window like liquid silver.

Memory lingered, of other nights standing just like this, gazing out at the vastness, imagining what lay across the land.

And now she knew what was there. The freedom. The friendships. The babies and her business.

A shadow flashed beyond the portico, drawing her gaze. Below her, she watched as a solitary man walked alone into the darkness.

The man who carried her heart.

And that's when the tears finally fell.

Although it felt as though her heart was ripping into torturous, bloody pieces, Cole was right.

In this house, she was a mere ghost of herself.

If she stayed, how long would it be before the life was sucked completely out of her? Before she drew into herself, retreated behind a puppet shell?

Before she no longer respected herself, was no longer the vibrant, sassy woman a man like Cole Martinez could love?

Chapter Fourteen

For the next two days, Johnny Cruz was indeed her shadow.

Raquel and Pilar had visited the palace and caught up on the news. Briana and Joseph were so in love, it almost hurt to watch them. There were changes aplenty at the palace. Briana's unrestrained laughter rang in the cavernous hallways, and the entire household looked on with loving indulgence as the blond princess did, said and acted as she pleased. There was a relaxed air to the regal abode, an easiness that was even reflected in the staff.

And everyone clucked over the royal baby who was due to make his entrance in the world in two months' time.

Although Raquel was happy for the prince and his princess, she couldn't get past the envy.

Or the sadness that had permeated her being since she'd said goodbye to Cole.

As she strolled through her family's showplace water gardens, her camera slung around her neck, she couldn't seem to build any enthusiasm to snap photos. Even the delicate beauty of a butterfly resting on a pale lavender lily failed to stir her.

From behind her came the sound of a man clearing his voice. Her heart leapt and she whirled.

But it wasn't Cole.

"Well, this is a fine greeting," Antonio Castillo said, his playboy, devil-may-care grin flashing. "I expect shrieks and kisses...swooning at the very least. And what do I get?" He clapped a hand to his heart as if mortally wounded. "A frown of disappointment."

Raquel laughed, feeling lighter than she had in days, and launched herself into Antonio's open arms.

"What is the spare heir doing paying a call in the middle of the day? Have you nothing better to do with your time? No starlets to woo? No car races or regattas in which to court danger?"

"I must tell you those choices sound very attractive, but today I am once again on the queen's mission."

Raquel arched a brow at his comically pained expression. "Mission?"

"*Si, mi bella.* It appears I am forever being dispatched to talk sense into the lovelorn. Which, if you think about it, is a perfectly ridiculous notion. I am *obviously* not the best man for the job given my aversion to commitment."

"Then why are you here?"

"The family and friends are concerned."

"About what?"

"You, Rapunzel." He tugged playfully at her shoulder-length hair. "You have shorn my silken ladder."

She grinned. "You were never a candidate for my fantasies and you know it."

"Ouch. I am losing my golden touch."

She punched him on the shoulder. "Tell me the truth, ladies' man. What do you think?" She fluffed the ends of her hair and executed a smooth pirouette.

His dark eyes twinkled in appreciation. Antonio was a connoisseur of women. And the closest thing to a brother she'd ever had.

"I like it, Rocky. Very chic. Very Paris."

"Thank you." She linked her arm through his. "Walk with me."

"We have a shadow," he noted, matching her slow strides.

Raquel glanced over her shoulder at her solemn bodyguard. "I have it on the best authority that we can trust Johnny to be discreet."

"Ah, but he reports to Cole. And Cole carries a gun that scares me right down to my Italian Loafers."

Just the mention of Cole's name sent her insides tumbling. "What does that have to do with anything?"

"I suspect if Cole thinks another man is making time with his lady, he'll shoot first and ask questions later."

"Why would you think I was his lady?"

Antonio grinned. "I know you, Rocky. And I know Martinez. The two of you are sending out sensual beacons bright enough to guide a sloop through the thickest mist. It has been that way since you returned together from France."

Something close to panic rushed through her veins. "Has anyone else noticed? I do not want to jeopardize his job."

"Nonsense. Loving you would never endanger his position. He is our most highly trained, highly trusted man of law. My own father, the king, cannot sing Cole's praises enough. And Don Carlos looks upon him as a surrogate son. Where would you get such a ridiculous idea of ruination?"

"From Cole."

"Ah, yes. You must understand, *bella*, that is a man

thing. Men *think* entirely too much, as opposed to women, who feel. And to answer your original question, no one has made the connection between the two of you. Dona Santiago, as well as the entire palace, think you are pining away for your artist beau.''

"Lucian?"

"I know it is a ridiculous notion. *They* do not know he flaked out the first week of your freedom escape."

But Antonio had known. Because he had visited. And as only a truly trusted friend would do, he'd kept her secrets and her whereabouts in confidence.

"In any case," he continued with an air of mock suffering, "*your* mother told *my* mother—the queen herself, mind you—that you are unhappy. She went to the king, who promptly dragged Joseph into the fray…and, of course, Princess Bri was right there to hear and *she* suggested *I* should be the lucky one to straighten you out and cheer you up."

Raquel laughed at the drama of his storytelling. "And you agreed without argument."

"Come now, Rocky. You know me better. I believe in the motto Live and let live. Alas, the queen had other ideas…." He glanced down at her, his eyes filled with gentle amusement. "And that woman terrifies me more than your Cole's gun. So tell all, *bella*. Why is there sadness in your eyes even when your mouth pretends to smile?"

She felt the wimpy tears sting her throat and eyes, and hated the weakness. Easing down on the stone bench that faced a tiered fountain spraying cool ripples of water into the man-made pond, she patted the seat beside her.

And when he joined her there, she told him everything. Her fears over losing her newfound freedom. The expectations of her family. The years of isolation when she was betrothed to his brother. Her life in France. Her thriving business. Her special bond with the babies...

Her love for Cole.

She talked until all her words, her hopes and her fears were spent.

Antonio, usually a kidder, listened in silence, his expression serious. A duck and her chicks swam past in the garden pond, bathing in the spray of the fountain.

"Do you not realize, Rocky, it is the walls of this estate that make you feel constrained, not Valldoria itself."

"But—"

"No. Listen to me. Living with your family, you are compelled to act the part of the good daughter. Yet you strain against those apron strings, especially now that you have had a taste of freedom."

A smile tugged at her mouth. "My mother has never worn an apron in her life." But Cole had. An image of him in her tiny kitchen, wearing the white bibbed smock trimmed in peonies flashed in her mind.

"Neither has mine," Antonio said. "But she still tugs the strings when she thinks she can get away with it."

"And sometimes you let her?"

"Would I be here if I did not?"

"Yes."

He chucked her lightly under the chin. "Smartypants. My point, Rocky, is you can have it all. Your freedom, here, with Cole, *and* your business. You are no longer a princess in training. Just a rich kid like me. The difference between us is that you are using your God-given talents to fulfill yourself. Through your photography. I am just a bum."

"Cut it out, Tony. I know your secrets, too." And they went much deeper than those of an idle playboy.

He flashed her a grin, skimmed right over the subject of himself, and like a dog with a coveted bone, continued to hammer home his point.

A point that she was already seeing in a different light. She'd been so caught up in worry, so shortsighted, she hadn't taken the time to fully examine the big picture.

If she stayed—with Cole—it would not be as a girl, but as a woman. A wealthy, independent woman who had no need to remain under her family's roof or subservient to their rules.

She would miss her friends, yes. But she had friends here. And here, she had Cole.

"We have beautiful babies in Valldoria." Antonio's voice softened. "And I know you love this country."

"Yes." She imagined all the places she could photograph the babies against the verdant landscape—perhaps even her own babies.

Hers and Cole's.

Tears spilled from her lids and her smile was watery as she laid her head against Tony's shoulder. "How did you get to be so smart?"

"It is merely a bluff."

"You're such a fraud, Tony. When you want to, you can be quite serious."

"Do not let that get around. I would not want to spoil my stellar reputation."

"Your secrets are safe with me. As they have always been." She wrapped her arms around his waist. "Thank you, Tony. Want to take a crack at Cole next?"

"Ah, no, *bella*. I butted into Joseph's life...and yours, because you are family—"

"And your mother threatened you, do not forget."

"Yes. That nudged me for certain. However, I will leave Cole to you."

"Thanks a lot. He is a stubborn man." She remembered what she'd gone through just to seduce him. Talking him into love and marriage would likely be an uphill, frustrating battle.

But he was worth it. *They* were worth it.

"I will give you one last piece of advice. Allow him the space to take care of the problems within your father's company. When the crisis is past, he will be more receptive to your persuasion."

"I can do that," she agreed.

Antonio winked. "Atta girl."

ANXIOUS TO SEE Cole, to convince him that they were indeed meant to be, Raquel had to consciously put the brakes on her desire. Antonio was right. Timing was crucial. And Cole needed the time to take care of business.

And once that was handled, he would have fewer barriers with which to resist her persuasion.

So she contented herself with searching out her mother.

She found the grand lady in the parlor, arranging freshly cut camellias and narcissi in a diamond-cut Baccarat vase, the spicy, heady scent of the flowers permeating the room.

"Ah, *mi hija.* What do you think?" She indicated the arrangement with a sweep of her hand.

Raquel astonished her mother by placing a kiss on her smooth cheek. "What I think is that you do not need to send Antonio to speak with me. If you worry over my disposition, ask me yourself."

Pilar looked unsettled for a moment, then sank onto the rose damask settee. "I was afraid you would not talk to me. You have always been so private. Keeping your thoughts to yourself."

Raquel sat opposite her mother. "You've never given me the opportunity to prove otherwise, *Madre,* you've never *asked* about my personal feelings."

"Only because it never occurred to me that you might wish for a confidante. You were always such a good child. You went along with everything, never objected."

"I did not have the right to object."

"We all have the right!"

"Do we?" Raquel asked softly, needing to put old ghosts to rest. "From birth you and Papa groomed me, planning for the day that your little girl would be a princess. That wasn't my dream, Mama. It was yours and Papa's. I was like the little beauty queen who runs the pageant circuit, paraded, taught, praised and held up for public approval.

"But rather than pageants, there were only schools, classes and public appearances. I learned adult skills, but not little-girl ones. I was lonely, Mama."

"You know you are your papa's angel."

"Do I? He has never once said aloud that he loves me."

The sound of an indrawn breath had her turning. Carlos Santiago stood in the doorway. Being a man unused to displaying emotions, he started to move away.

"Papa," Raquel said. "Do not go. Please. Join us."

He stepped into the parlor as though it were filled with venomous snakes. He was a man used to command. And his reluctance clearly indicated the atmosphere in this room was out of his realm of expertise.

She decided to let him off the hook, knew he would never say the words of his own accord. "I know you love me, Papa."

He folded his arms across his chest, but the moisture in his eyes betrayed him. "Frilly words are the woman's responsibility," he said gruffly.

"Oh, be quiet, Carlos," Pilar admonished, showing who truly ran this household. Without giving him another glance, she turned back to Raquel. "It was not our intention to rob you of your childhood."

"I know." She reached out, covering her mother's hand. Although Pilar wasn't a woman used to warm displays of emotion, of touching, she turned her palm up, squeezing.

"We have missed much, my daughter. And now I fear you are about to tell me you are leaving again."

Oh, it hurt. So many years wasted in the sterility of protocol. Maybe they could make up for it—from a safe distance of a few miles, she thought.

From the distance of Cole's house or even a home they would build together.

It may be a touch-and-go thing to get him to open his heart, to set aside his stubbornness, but it would be worth the battle.

Because at last Raquel knew what was truly important, knew that home was where the heart was.

And hers was with Cole...and with the fragile rebuilding of a relationship with her family.

"Actually," she said, glancing at both her parents. "I am thinking I will stay. My business is such that its roots can be planted anywhere, on any soil. And I've come to realize that Valldoria is very fertile soil."

"Fertile?" Carlos roared, hearing nothing past that single word. "*Dios!* Do not tell me you are pregnant.

Is that the reason you are moping so lately?" As he ranted, he paced. "Your *madre* has spoken to the queen—"

"Papa?"

"I will kill that artist *diablo*—"

"Papa." Her voice rose.

He halted. "What?"

"I am not pregnant."

"Oh." His shoulders relaxed, his burnished skin turning ruddy. *"Bueno."*

"And nothing ever came of my relationship with Lucian."

"It didn't?" He sounded both relieved and surprised.

"No. But I *am* in love. And if he'll have me, I intend to ask Cole Martinez to marry me."

Pilar sucked in a breath with a happy murmur, thanking every blessed saint she could think to name.

Carlos went absolutely still, like the lull in an angry storm that is not yet spent. "You...he is a—"

Raquel held up a hand in warning. "Think carefully before you speak, Papa. Before you say something we will both regret. He is the man I love."

Slowly, carefully, Carlos stepped forward. Stopping in front of her, he reached out and touched her shoulder-length hair. Traditionally, the Santiago women did not cut their hair, and they certainly didn't streak it with red highlights.

There was no censure in his gaze, though, nor in his fatherly touch. "Does he return your love, daughter?"

Raquel shrugged. Here her certainty was a little shaky. "I believe he does. He has some misguided worries that I intend to set him straight on, though."

"You have changed much, *mi hija*. You have my blessings. I must ask one thing, though."

"What is that?"

"When you provide me with grandchildren, will they forever be bedecked in the spoils of the garden?"

Raquel laughed and hugged her father. "Not forever, Papa. Only in their young years."

Carlos glanced at his wife. "Clear the walls of the estate, madam. I have a feeling our taste in fine art is about to undergo a drastic change."

SITTING IN FRONT of the isolated warehouse, Cole had plenty of time on his hands to think. He'd thought breaking it off with Raquel would suddenly bring all his concentration back.

He'd been wrong. Her image kept dancing in his mind, her scent haunting his senses as though he'd absorbed it into his own skin.

But the strongest image he would remember for as long as he lived, was the one of her in the window, the fingertips of one hand pressed to her lips, the other pressed to the panes of the glass.

Dear God, it had taken every ounce of control he possessed not to race back in that house, to sweep her in his arms and beg her to let him love her, to protect her, to set her free.

He wanted to be the knight to climb her tower.

And it was these raw emotions that were causing his shoddy handling of his job. He'd blown it, big time. He'd been thinking with his hormones and his heart instead of his head.

Thank God it wasn't too late to straighten matters out.

Still, he couldn't believe he'd dismissed Lucian Delgado as a threat. He'd simply categorized the guy as an old beau.

An old beau who'd wanted Raquel for her fortune, he realized now.

Cole should have investigated the guy sooner, probed into his background and family. Had he done so, he'd have made the connection between Lucian and Maurice Patillas, known they were cousins.

Hell, Lucian had shown up in France the day after the photo had turned up missing. And Cole had screwed up, never made the connection, too wrapped up in his own wants to think like the trained operative that he was.

But he was on track now. They'd traced the warehouse full of explosives to Maurice Patillas. Now all he needed was for the guy to show up, to catch him dead to rights so there would be no loopholes a slick lawyer could get around.

And because he couldn't be sure when—or if—Patillas would show, he didn't want to expend the manpower in case his hunch turned out to be a wild-goose chase. He'd call in backup later. For now, he'd just wait.

And try like hell to keep his mind on business.

A shadow whispered over the hood of his unmarked sedan and gravel crunched. Adrenaline shot his system into high gear.

He wasn't alone.

Chapter Fifteen

The private telephone in Raquel's bedroom rang. There weren't too many people who had this number. Family, friends...and Cole.

Heart racing, she snatched up the receiver.

"Yes?"

"Senorita Santiago?"

Her spirits sank. It wasn't Cole. "Speaking."

"This is Pedro from His Majesty's Royal Palace. Please remain calm."

Those very words sent her insides into a flash-point mass that was the polar opposite of calm.

"What is it? What's wrong?"

"Please. You must not panic."

"Then spit it out, damn it! You are scaring the hell out of me."

There was the slightest pause on the other end of the line. Obviously she'd shocked this royal guard with her outburst.

"Senior Martinez has sustained a wound and has requested that you be summoned to his side."

"Oh, *Madre de Dios!* How bad? Is he okay? Where is he?"

"If you have something to write on, I will recite the address."

Her hands shook so badly she could hardly get the bedside drawer open. Paper. She needed paper. And a pen. Heart pumping, she upended the drawer, scrambled on the floor, retrieving the pencil. "Go!"

Kneeling on the plush wool rug by the bed, she anchored the paper with her knee and scribbled the information. It was barely legible. Without a hard surface, her pen penetrated the flimsy paper making ones look like sixes and twos look like threes.

It didn't matter. Even without the benefit of the written numbers, she would find him. If nothing else, her adrenaline and love would guide her there.

She wanted to ask more questions. Didn't want to take the time. "I'm on my way," she panted, unable to draw a decent breath. If something happened to Cole before she could get to him, she imagined she'd lie down and die right alongside him. "Does Johnny know?"

Pedro paused. "Johnny?"

"Cruz!" She nearly shouted. "Johnny Cruz—oh, forget it, I don't have time to find him. Tell Cole I'm coming."

"DO NOT SHOOT, *amigo*. I am unarmed."

Cole swore and lowered his weapon. "What the hell are you doing sneaking up on me like that, Antonio? I nearly blew your head off."

"I was not sneaking," Antonio said with mild affront. "I saw the sedan parked here, and in case you were on a stakeout, I did not want to come speeding down the lane in the Ferrari and give you away."

"If you realized I was on a stakeout you should have stayed away."

"I said *in case,* Martinez. With the wave of melancholy sweeping the land, how was I to know you were not simply indulging in a pity party yourself. After all, it appears you are alone. Not the standard procedure, if you ask me."

"Nobody asked you."

"Ah, I see you are as surly and unfriendly as ever. I will bid you *adios.*"

"Wait." Cole knew he was acting like a jerk, but he was damned jumpy. And Antonio was a friend. One of the few he had. "As long as you're here, you might as well keep me company. I'm sick of my own."

Antonio grinned. "Figured as much. I've just come from…" his words trailed off as the sound of an approaching car disturbed the stillness.

Both men ducked out of sight behind the fender of the white sedan while still keeping the warehouse in sight.

"By your lack of surprise, I take it this guy has an engraved invitation for the shoot-'em-up *fiesta?*"

"Yeah," Cole said. "Maurice Patillas. He's pissed off at Santiago for canning him. Has a penchant for delivering packages that have a nasty habit of exploding."

Tony gave a silent whistle. "So what are your plans?"

"Now that he's here, I'll call for backup. In the meantime, we watch."

Cole punched in Cruz's number. The line barely rang.

"The bird's landed," he said when Cruz picked up. "You located Delgado yet?" Cole saw Antonio's brow raise in recognition of the name.

"The pretty boy's in custody," Cruz said. "We've got big problems, though. I didn't even have to go looking for Lucian. He found me. He claims Patillas is crazy. Says his cousin plans to nab Raquel."

Cole felt icy fingers of fear slither down his spine. Razor sharp, his senses went on alert. "Find her. Tie her up if you have to, but don't let her out of your sight."

"She's missing," Cruz said baldly. "Damn it, I don't know how she got past us."

The sound of rubber burning up asphalt snagged his attention.

A sporty green Mercedes. With Raquel at the wheel.

"Bring in the troops," he snapped. "She just showed up at the warehouse." He disconnected the cell phone.

His first instinct was to shout, to race down there and snatch her out of harm's way. He was going to wring her neck.

Before he could act on instinct, Antonio clapped a hand at his shoulder, swearing softly.

Too late.

Patillas had come from behind the warehouse and had a gun jammed in Raquel's throat.

She was his hostage. Cole's blood turned to ice, and all his careful training went by the wayside. He jerked away from Antonio's restraining hand and stood.

"Think, man," Antonio said. "Fools rush in, and you are no fool. You need backup."

He spared a glance at his friend. "You see any soldiers around here that I happened to miss?" he asked sarcastically, his insides screaming for action, his head telling him Antonio was right.

"I am not a soldier, but you ought to know I am

handy with an automatic pistol. You trained me yourself.''

"Great, just what I need. A civilian to contend with—a *royal* civilian. Forget it, Tony. I don't want the liability."

"Tough tamales, buddy. You need assistance and I'm all you've got. And right now, I'm probably thinking a lot clearer than you. You want to fight me on this, we'll square off later. In the meantime, there is a damsel in distress who happens to be important to *both* of us."

Cole wasn't sure how Antonio had found out about his feelings for Raquel, but he didn't have time for pleasant chats. They needed action. Now.

Antonio's love of danger and fearless spirit were actually a stabilizer. The younger prince was a man Cole could trust to watch his back.

Reaching in the car, he retrieved a spare forty-five and checked the clip.

"We'll go in low, check the windows. Don't make a move until I give the go-ahead."

BEING SHELTERED all her life, Raquel had no experience with this type of danger. Having a lethal-looking gun pointed right at her heart was a sobering, frightening, enlightening experience.

This was reality. This was truly the meaning of having one's free will taken from them.

Panic shook her from head to toe, trembled in her voice. There was no help for it.

"Pedro, I assume?"

"No. Maurice Patillas, at your service, heiress."

"And Cole has not been injured, has he?" Anger over the ruse—and her own stupidity—went a long way in steadying her nerves.

Maurice cackled, causing Raquel to frown. He sounded like a man who'd slipped over the edge of sanity.

"I knew you would come if your lawman lover was mentioned."

"What makes you think he's my lover?"

"Now, now, rich girl. Would you come running from your fancy house for just anybody? Besides, Lucian told me you were sleeping with Martinez."

"Lucian?" Confusion threatened to shake her tenuous hold on control. "Why would Lucian tell you such a thing?" Memory flashed like a strobe. In France. She'd wanted to shake up Cole, had told Lucian that Cole was her lover.

"Ah, *senorita*, I see I must update you and make formal introductions. Lucian Delgado is my cousin. It was our plan months ago that the two of you would run off together and wed. Had that happened, there would have been no need for the measures that I have been forced to take."

"Lucian is in on this?"

"That fool could not find his way out of a paper bag. If you want to know the truth of the matter, I suspect he is gay." He cackled again. "He was very relieved when Don Carlos disinherited you. My cousin did not want to marry you."

She should have felt insulted. Instead, she felt relieved. "Is that what this is about? Money?"

"*Excelente!* Go to the head of the class for brains." He banged his hand against the wall in an imitation of clapping. "Of course it is about money. What is due to me. I am paid peanuts at that smelly harbor, yet if it was not for me, the great Santiagos would not make a cent. So what is the harm in padding my pockets?"

Raquel didn't like the way he was waving that gun. She hoped to God he knew enough about weapons so as not to shoot it by accident.

She needed a plan, needed to get her bearings. The inside of the warehouse was stacked with sticks of dynamite. It was a storage facility for the blasting that went on in the platinum mines.

Dear heaven, if Maurice discharged that gun within these explosive surroundings, he'd very likely blow their country off the face of the map.

There was a wooden bin filled with sulfur just to her right. A germ of an idea formulated, but she needed a distraction, needed to buy a little time.

Since Maurice seemed happy enough to brag about himself, she gave him a nudge. "Actually, Maurice...may I call you by your Christian name?"

He shrugged his assent and the gun wavered. Raquel flinched and used the show of fear to inch a few feet to the right.

"I am no longer disinherited. I have money I can give you. If you will allow me to retrieve my purse, I will write you a check." She made it another two steps.

"You think I am *estupido?* The bank can refuse to honor a check. No, I want the high and mighty Santiago to pay for his precious daughter's return. And stand still," he barked.

She thrust her hands behind her and leaned against the metal shelving, her fingertips brushing the splintery wood of the sulfur container.

"Sorry," she said, her voice trembling in earnest. "When I am frightened, I fidget and pace."

Maurice frowned. "I do not mean to frighten you."

The man was certifiable...*loco.* But his preoccupation had given her the opportunity she needed. Her hand closed around a fist of sulfur. Now, if she could just get close enough to fling it in his eyes, she could make a run for it.

Searching for a means of exit, her eyes widened.

Cole and Antonio stood behind Maurice, toward the back of the warehouse, weapons pointing toward the ceiling.

Her heart hammered in her chest. She wanted to allow her gaze to linger, but she didn't want to give away his position. Just knowing he was there steadied her, gave her courage.

She'd suggested Cole take her on as an assistant. Now was her chance to prove herself worthy of the position.

With Antonio here as an indisputably credible witness, she wanted to make sure Maurice spilled as much incriminating information as possible so the case against him would be airtight.

How dare this weasel try to blow up her father.

How dare he extend that threat to Cole!

She forced her attention back to Maurice, made every effort to keep her voice level.

"How did you get my private telephone number? Did Lucian give it to you? And was *he* the one who broke into my house?" *Fool,* she chided herself. She shouldn't have made so many inquiries in a row.

But Maurice actually looked pleased to answer the questions. Cole, however, was giving her deadly serious signals that were fairly comical if she could afford to take a good look.

Apparently he wanted her to shut up.

She ignored him. He might as well learn right now that she no longer intended to do as she was told.

Maurice propped a casual hand on his hip, the gun pointing toward the floor rather than at her heart.

"Lucian is a great disappointment to me. I thought I could count on him to help, but as I told you, he wears panties instead of briefs."

Raquel's jaw nearly dropped. Actually, he'd only said he *suspected* the artist had feminine tendencies.

"He did not hand over the telephone number, but it was conveniently in his black book from when the two of you were slipping around like star-crossed lovers." His laughter had a desperate sadness to it. "We are cousins, but he could have been like a son to me. I caught him wearing a dress. Oh, he said it was practice for a play, but I knew better. I told him I would ruin him. He is a fraidy-cat, it was easy enough to make him break into your house."

"Why did you have him steal the picture of Cole?" She knew Cole and Antonio were moving forward. She cautioned herself not to glance in their direction, not to give them away.

"I am a fair man. I like to give my opponent a sporting chance. Martinez was to have found the photo and understood its message so he could intercept the letter bomb before it reached Don Carlos. I loathe your father, but he is no good to me dead."

"And neither would I be, Maurice. Despite what you say about Lucian, I have strong feelings for him." The lie tripped off her tongue smoothly. "I will give you the money you deserve. You may even accompany me to the bank. That way you can see that there are no surprises."

He scratched his dark forehead. She took a step closer.

Cole and Antonio closed in from behind.

Maurice was lost in thought. Distracted. It was now or never.

She brought her hand from behind her back.

Cole saw her intentions too late. He wanted to scream, but his vocal cords were suddenly paralyzed.

Black sulfur flew like locusts straight for Maurice's eyes.

Maurice howled. The gun went skidding as Antonio executed an impressive body block.

Cole, knees bent, weapon palmed in both hands, fought like hell not to pull the trigger. The urge to kill the sick bastard lodged in his mind like a terminal disease. This scum had threatened Raquel, could have snuffed out her life if he'd so much as sneezed while holding the gun.

The cords on his arms stood out. Sweat beaded his forehead. His fingers flexed.

The warehouse doors burst open, the Royal Guard in full uniform surrounding them, weapons aimed.

And still, Cole didn't take his hand off the trigger. Just a little squeeze.

"Cole?"

Raquel's soft, trembling voice penetrated the mist of rage. He glanced down, saw her hand on his arm, the black residue of sulfur coating her fingers and his shirt.

He eased up, flicked on the forty-five's safety. "Get this piece of garbage out of here," he said, noting that Cruz stood just behind his elbow, awaiting instructions.

Cole turned away, afraid he was about to embarrass himself in front of his men. He felt his emotions roil, tried to get them under control.

He failed miserably.

Without tenderness or caution, he whirled and snatched Raquel into his arms, holding her against his heart, his hands racing over her back and her arms as though checking for injuries.

"God, spitfire, I'm sorry. This is all my fault. I screwed up." He punctuated his words with kisses and featherlight touches. "Are you all right? Did he hurt you?"

"I'm fine, Cole."

She raised her hands to his face…and incredibly, she burst into laughter. He frowned. Was she hysterical? He'd seen plenty of victims fall apart after the danger was past.

"Shhh, you'll be fine, *querida*."

"Oh, I like it when you call me that."

He bent his knees so his face was on a level with hers. "I have used the endearment hundreds of times."

"No. Only once. In France, when you were concerned that I was repressing memories of horrible things. Does only danger and horror bring out this loving side of you?"

Cole was sure he had missed a vital part of the conversation. She made little sense.

He looked at Antonio for help. Male help.

The young prince merely grinned like a fool.

Cole straightened and gathered Raquel in his arms. "Let's get you out of here. All these guns around this much dynamite makes me nervous."

He made it out the door and several yards away before his screaming emotions tumbled out in a rush. He pulled her to a halt, yanked her around to face him.

"Damn it, Raquel, don't ever scare me like that again. I nearly died when that creep had the gun at your neck." His voice scraped against his raw throat.

She cupped his face, both amusement and love shining in her velvet-brown eyes. "I love you, too, Cole Martinez."

He blinked. "I didn't say anything about love," he hedged, a smile pulling at his mouth.

"Maybe not with your mouth, but your eyes and your touch are shouting loud enough to wake the dead."

Softly now, his smile grew. "That loud?"

She pressed her lips to his. "Pretty close." She wiped her hands on her figure-hugging capri pants, then used the backs of her fingers to rub at his cheeks. "I have dirtied you with the sulfur, and the black smudges are making it difficult for me to keep a straight face."

Her concentration on her task, coupled with her touch and her breathtaking beauty nearly slayed him. "I'm about to break my own code, spitfire."

Her hands paused, resting against his shoulders. "What's that?"

"I'm going to beg you to stay with me." When she opened her mouth, he placed a fingertip across her lips. "I want you more than anything, *querida*. I love you. I'll quit my job, go anywhere you want."

A lump formed in her throat. "You would give that up for me?"

"In a heartbeat."

Tears filled her eyes. She shook her head.

"Please, baby. Don't say no." He felt like he was fighting for his life. If she left him now, he wouldn't survive. "I—"

"Hush, Cole Martinez. If you continue to talk, I cannot ask you to marry me. To live with me here in Valldoria. The home of our birth."

He felt his heart pound. She'd just offered him his heart's desire, yet...

"Marriage is a big step. I have prestige in my job, I

own a home and I receive a substantial salary, but I'm far from rich. What can I give you that you don't already have? Or that you can't get for yourself?"

"Babies," she said softly, seriously. "A little girl who will never feel the need to let down her hair from the tower wall to be rescued. And a little boy who will have the heart of a knight, yet the strength to let his ladylove stand on her own."

He swallowed. Unsure if he could speak, he kissed her instead, told her without words how he loved her, how she humbled him.

She ran her hands down his arms, squeezed his hands.

"And you can give me these babies right here in Valldoria," she whispered against his lips. "Because I've finally realized what home is really about. It's about the heart. And mine is here with you."

He'd never felt so pumped up, so empowered, so damned lucky in all his life. "I love you."

"I know. And that alone has set me free." She gave him a mock frown. "I will have to insist on the marriage part, though. Living in sin is pushing rebellion way too far."

He laughed, lifted her off her feet and swung her around. On the second revolution, they both noticed Antonio leaning against the fender of Raquel's moss-green Mercedes.

"Tony, my friend. Will you do me the honor of being the best man at my wedding?"

"Now wait just a minute," Raquel interrupted. "You have not yet formally agreed to my proposal."

"I didn't?"

"No."

"Just as well, the man's supposed to do the asking."

"Careful, my love, I have a great right hook, and my accuracy with sulfur is dead on."

"You're a scary woman. My answer is, yes. I would give my soul to marry you."

She grinned. "A simple yes will do. No need to offer body parts."

"I'm a sucker for a smart-mouth woman."

She winked. "I know. And back to the wedding plans, by rights, I think Antonio should stand up for *me*. After all, there has always been a special bond between us." She glanced at both Cole and Antonio, feeling so blessed she could hardly contain her emotions.

"If I can jilt a prince and marry the knight, I can surely have the spare heir stand at my side."

Cole threw back his head and laughed, pulling Raquel back into his arms, where he intended to keep her for a good long time.

Antonio pretended horror. "You know I adore you, Rocky, but I draw the line at wearing a dress. So I will accept your honor, Cole. On one condition."

"And that is?"

"I must urge you to hurry with these wedding plans. All this commitment stuff is touching, but it is giving me the willies. I find I have a major itch to head for my yacht and set sail for less-intense, more-carefree harbors."

Chelsa Lawrence sat on the enclosed porch of her rented bungalow, her arms wrapped around her two daughters. A storm had slammed into the Mediterranean coast, fierce and unforgiving, turning the small island of San Alegra into a state of unstable anticipation. The surf pounded and the wind howled. It was almost midnight and Chelsa knew the girls should've been in bed hours ago, but the fear of tidal waves and rooftops blown off by winds had both little girls huddled close, watching the specter of nature unfold.

Their imaginations were vivid, as was their mother's. After all, the children's books Chelsa wrote, The Adventures of Water Babies, were fashioned after her own girls, Emily and Sophie. Chelsa marveled at their little minds, their endless questions, and used them in the stories she wrote.

But tonight her thoughts weren't on sweet, innocent stories. Perhaps it was the ferocious intensity of the storm, but she felt a sense of foreboding.

Her arm tightened. She would keep her daughters safe.

"Mommy, you're squishing the bref out of me."

"Sorry, Sophie." She eased her grip on her four-year-old.

"Momma?" This time it was Emily's quiet voice. "Do you think that boat will hit the rocks?"

"Hmm?" She hadn't noticed a boat.

Sophie wiggled out of her hold and perched forward on the bench. "Pirates," she whispered.

"There's no such thing as pirates," Emily admonished. Being six, she felt her knowledge was much superior to her younger sister's.

"Uh-huh! Member Hook? And Tinkerbell?"

"That's just movies, silly. Right, Momma?" Superior she might be, but still a little girl who got scared.

"Yes, sweetie. It's just a movie. But it's fun to imagine." Of course, there were still pirates roaming the seas, but none so dramatic as the movies might depict.

"See!" Sophie chirped and rested pudgy hands on equally pudgy knees. Emily rolled her eyes because her little sister still didn't get it.

Chelsa stood. Pirate or not, that boat was in grave danger. The sea roiled and spat, tossing the sleek craft around like a rubber duck in a washing machine. Waves crashed over the rocks that jutted maybe fifty yards offshore, cascading over the sides in a beard of frothy foam. It appeared as though the skipper was attempting to head for the beach, but the gusty winds and churning swells thwarted his efforts.

Her heart started to pound and adrenaline kicked in. The beach was pitch-black, illuminated only by the light of a partial moon against the foamy crest of the waves. The power was out in the house, and the phone lines were down. If the ship crashed, there would be no way to call for help.

But then, Chelsa shouldn't even be considering calling for help. She had no business getting involved, especially since there was no telling who was aboard that ship. Including a modern-day pirate.

And at all costs, she had her children to think about. Their safety.

In a matter of two weeks or less, their lives could very well be in danger. All of their lives.

A sinister blast of wind sprayed sand and sea salt, testing the strength of the screen door. The pounding of angry water against unforgiving rock superseded the sound of splintering wood as the yacht lost its control against nature and slammed into the rocks. Like straw in a dust devil, debris scattered, whirling, projected into the air, flung high and wide at the mercy of the storm.

And in that instant before impact, Chelsa saw someone dive for safety. The girls were jumping now, both terrified and excited.

"Momma! The rocks breaked the boat!" Sophie screamed.

"Momma! A man jumped over the side!"

"Yes," Chelsa said, her hand hesitating at the screen door, indecision screaming within her.

"Go get him, Momma."

"Wait," she said. "Hush, now." She had to think, didn't quite know what to do.

"But he's not swimming. He's just floating," Emily said.

"You gotta get him, Momma," Sophie said, her solemn blue eyes round with worry. "Willy can't save him in the big waves."

She was talking about the whale in *Free Willy*. Her children watched entirely too many movies, Chelsa decided.

And they expected her to be a heroine. She'd never felt less like a heroine in her life. But with two sets of expectant, round eyes looking up at her, she had little choice.

"Stay right here. Both of you. Don't move a muscle, do you understand?" At their twin nods, Chelsa kicked off her sandals and raced across the cool sand.

She saw him surface. Like a bodysurfer with the aid of unseen hands, he rode the crest of a wave, the momentum dumping him onshore right at her feet. Battling winds that slashed at her clothes, whipping her hair in a wild frenzy, she flipped him over, gripped him beneath his arms and tugged. Wet and shaking, adrenaline lent her strength as she dragged him free of the fierce current.

The horrendous weather was like an omen, an evil one. She felt exposed, yet knew she was overreacting. Her life was in chaos, though, and the weight of it was sucking her down, much like the ocean was swallowing the remains of the boat.

She set those thoughts aside for the moment and checked her beached sailor. He was breathing, thank goodness, but his eyes were closed.

"Can you hear me?" she shouted over the force of the storm.

He didn't respond. Unconscious. And no wonder. With the way that yacht had exploded against the rocks, it was a miracle he was even drawing a breath.

"Is he dead?"

"Is there any blood?"

Her head whipped around. "I thought I told you girls to stay on the porch!"

"Sophie got scared," Emily blamed.

"Nuh-uh!"

"Stop it, both of you. I don't need this right now."

The girls flanked her, wrapping their arms around her in apology.

Chelsa took a steadying breath. "Sorry, girls. Momma didn't mean to shout."

"That's okay," Emily said. "What are you going to do with the man?"

"Get him to the house, I guess." And get her daughters out of the open, exposed, where anyone might see or harm them. Fear over being seen doubled her determination. Stretched out on the wet sand, he appeared to be over six feet. And he outweighed her by a good eighty pounds.

But there was no one else to rely on for help, a truth she'd become all too familiar with lately.

With the hem of her dress swirling around her ankles, threatening to trip her, she waded into the tide and snagged a piece of canvas before the surf could carry it out again. She didn't know a lot about fancy yachts, but it was obvious this was part of the sail. Once again, she realized this man should be counting his blessings. It would take horrendous force to rip this sturdy canvas. It was a wonder this man's body wasn't in the same shape.

Praying she wasn't setting herself up for a lawsuit over moving an individual who might have a neck injury, she rolled him onto the canvas and tugged.

His feet cut deep furrows in the sand as she back-tracked the hundred or so yards to the bungalow. Straining, her shoulder muscles feeling as if they were on fire, she managed to drag him into the house—though the porch steps scraping along his back gave her grief and made her wince. The girls were more hindrance than help, but she didn't have the heart to tell them so. They were so proud of themselves for doing their part.

For an instant, she considered making him comfortable outside on the screened-in porch, but that offended her ingrained southern hospitality. Her own mother would've had a fit.

By the time she had him settled in the bed, she was exhausted. Candles burned, casting a shadowy glow over his still features.

When she got a good look, she sucked in a breath.

Oh, no. Handsome as sin. Easily recognizable.

Her heart raced as she charged to the window and jerked down the shade.

"Emily, lock the doors. Sophie, go with your sister."

"Why—"

"Just do as I say. And stay inside."

The last thing she needed was the possibility of lurking photographers, some hungry journalist snapping pictures of her girls. And where this man went, paparazzi were sure to follow.

She took another breath and looked back at the unconscious, soaked man lying on her bed. Hands trembling, she fisted them, and ordered herself to relax.

There was work to be done still—the highly interesting task of undressing this virile, exquisitely thrilling celebrity.

The royal Don Juan who set both Latin and American women's hearts aflutter.

Even in repose, he oozed charm. And the instant she touched his bare skin, she learned that a harried mother of two from Mississippi wasn't in any way immune to the magnetic draw of Prince Antonio Castillo of Valldoria.